MW01656840

THE GIRL IN HIDEAWAY PARK

A HIDEAWAY ISLE THRILLER

KELLY UTT

STANDARDS OF STARLIGHT

The Girl in Hideaway Park is a work of fiction. Any references to historical events, real people, or real places are used fictitiously. Other names, characters, places, and events are products of the author's imagination, and any resemblance to actual events or places or persons, living or dead, is entirely coincidental.

2020 Standards of Starlight Paperback Edition

www.standardsofstarlight.com

ISBN: 978-1-952893-10-0

Cover art by Elizabeth Mackey

PART I

ISLAND GIRLS

1

PREMONITION

BASIA

I love Lottie Callaway with all my heart. She's my girlfriend, my partner, and my lover. She's a bright young thing, passionate and wild with a belly full of fire. Not to mention, Lottie is stunningly beautiful. I don't toss that compliment around lightly. She's a magnificent creature to behold, all long legs and sultry, sun-kissed skin.

She turns heads everywhere she goes. She certainly turned mine.

I reach over and tuck a strand of long, blonde hair behind Lottie's ear as I muse, watching the sun illuminate her face and highlight the fine details. We're seated at an outdoor table on the patio of a waterfront burger joint downtown. It's lunchtime on Hideaway Isle, and the place is crowded. Lottie is scrolling through social media on her smartphone as we wait for our food, her legs crossed. I order a black and blue burger, topped with blue cheese crumbles, lettuce, and onion. She chooses a veggie burger with chipotle sauce, avocado, and slaw. That's my girl--

hip and health conscious at the same time. She kicks one foot absentmindedly, barely noticing my touch.

"Babe," I say. "We're eating cheeseburgers in paradise."

Lottie chuckles. She knows how obsessed I am with Jimmy Buffet, so she gets the song reference without me having to explain.

I play old Buffet music more than Lottie would probably like. It reminds me of my dad. My *real* dad. I don't remember much about him-- he left before I was even old enough for Kindergarten-- but for some reason, Jimmy Buffet stands out in my mind. That and the old-school pipe he used to smoke with loose, cherry-scented tobacco. The kind that came in a pouch. Pa, as I called him, always told me that my grandfather smoked the same pipe and the same cherry-scented tobacco. I wouldn't know. Grandpa Guthrie didn't come around. I guess the men in my family are more comfortable walking away. Despite my lonesome past, Buffet's Margaritaville restaurant is my absolute favorite place to eat when I go to Key West. They have a huge screen in the dining room where they show live Jimmy Buffet concerts on repeat. It's glorious. Not to mention, their key lime pie is to die for. I hop over there every chance I get. Lottie often tags along. Our schedules are usually flexible.

Hideaway Isle is a nice spot to call home. Key West is close enough to visit frequently, yet far enough that we maintain our own distinctive island vibes and attractions. I'm not from here, originally, but I like to think I chose well when I packed up and headed south from Wisconsin on my eighteenth birthday. I'd heard about a group of creative, bohemian types called the Rainbow Family and their Rainbow Gatherings. I joined them, which eventually led me all the way to South Florida. It wasn't the most conventional path, but I like to think I landed in the right place. I like to think I belong here, on Hideaway Isle with Lottie. It's good to belong.

"We sure are, Basia, babe," Lottie mumbles, still focused on her phone. "Cheeseburger in paradise… Heaven on Earth with an onion slice…"

She tilts her head as she sings the words softly. It's already a perfect day. Lottie's sweet voice makes it even better. I could stay here on this patio with her forever if she'd let me.

It was Lottie who first told me that Jimmy Buffet had written novels. I had no idea but was excited to find out. Lottie stumbled upon that tidbit-- and other random Buffet trivia I didn't know about-- while researching my favorite beach bum online.

I smile at her, appreciating the interest she takes in me.

We were supposed to meet Lottie's sister, Margot Callaway, and her boyfriend, Rags Bertram, here. They bailed at the last minute. Something about their retriever, Cap, having rolled in a foul substance at the dog park. It happens. Whip-poor-will, the scraggly brown mutt I had as a kid, used to do the same thing. She'd make a beeline for anything nasty that she could smear all over herself. It was gross, and dogs are strange. Margot and Rags promised to catch up with us later, which is just as well. Lottie and I need some alone time to decompress after everything that's happened lately. The four of us are scheduled to have dinner soon, anyway, with Lottie and Margot's newfound brother, Puck Reed, and his pregnant girlfriend, Chely Dern. We're all still getting to know each other.

It's been a wild summer, and there's plenty of summer left to go. Believe me when I tell you we've been through some fresh hell.

Lottie went from feeling she was alone to losing a grandfather she had largely taken for granted. Even though she didn't see him often, she loved Grandpa Vern dearly. His loss hit her hard. Immediately after, she reconnected with her sister and gained a bonus brother that neither of them knew existed. All of this happened around the same time we were held hostage by a mad man. Lottie was tied to a chair and threatened with bodily harm. It was intense.

I know. It sounds like a soap opera when I tell it that way. I don't know any other way to tell it. Our summer has been dramatic. And I haven't even mentioned the accident at Lottie's boat tour company. My only consolation is that Lottie and I are in this crazy life together. I'm careful to avoid making premature assumptions, but I suspect we're committed for the long haul.

I wasn't looking for a romantic relationship when I met Lottie last year. In fact, I tried to dodge her advances because I hadn't come out yet. I was still dating boys back then, letting them kiss me even though it turned my stomach when their slimy lips met my own, their hot, foul breath on my face. Yuck. I guess I was still hoping I could somehow hide the fact that I'm gay.

I can say it now.

I'm gay. Gay, gay, gay. Queer as a two dollar bill.

It may sound like a simple enough thing, but for me, the proclamation is huge progress.

I've known I was different for as long as I can remember, but before I met Lottie, I wasn't able to face up to the reality of my sexuality and what it meant for my future. Where I come from in small-town Midwestern USA, us gays-- as they like to call us-- are often shamed and ridiculed. I guess it was lucky that I pass for straight most of the time. My life would have taken an even more severe change for the worse if people at home knew what I was. *Who* I was. *Who I am*. It's a shame, really. I can't help being gay any more than I can help having blue eyes and blonde hair. I don't know the science, but I feel it. This is me. I was made this way. I came into the world gay, despite my mama and pa's wishes. I'm pretty sure they'd change me if they could. If they knew about my gayness and if they knew how to rid me of it, they'd do it. In a heartbeat. It's depressing to think about.

None of that mattered to Lottie. I tried telling her I couldn't be with her, and that no one knew my orientation. My efforts were in vain. Resisting her was futile. She literally kissed away my tears. She made me feel things I'd only fantasized about during my most private moments. In contrast to the disgusting experience of kissing boys, making out with Lottie showed me what real passion and lust-- *and love*-- was supposed to feel like. That feisty island girl came in like a wrecking ball and plumb rocked my world. I mean that in a good way. She opened me up. She helped me blossom.

We're young, and we don't know what we don't know, but we've chosen to stick together for the foreseeable future. It's easy when we're together. There's a flow between Lottie and me that's hard to describe with words. We can simply be with each other. No criticisms. No cumbersome expectations. Just being. I like it-- and her-- a lot.

I doubt I'm the only person who wants a little more ease in their day-to-day existence. Life is complicated enough, what with trying to earn a living to survive and get through the rat race unscathed. It's a slog. My mama used to say that it's hard, but it's fair. I don't know about the fair part. It's hard, sure enough. Who needs unnecessary relationship drama on top of all that? I know I don't. *No, sir.* I had plenty of drama growing up. Enough to last the rest of my days. If I could sign up for an easy button, you bet your ass I'd do it.

"What?" Lottie asks when she finally feels me staring at her.

A gentle breeze moves a potted palm nearby. The plant sways to the rhythm as a small black bird balances on one of its fronds, teetering.

I've been admiring Lottie's beauty for the better part of five minutes now. She's been too preoccupied with her phone to notice. The way she bites her bottom lip when she concentrates is almost too much. It makes me think naughty thoughts about those lips and where she could place them on my naked body. She's such a sensual lover. I close my eyes for a few seconds and smile as I savor the thought.

"Just looking at you," I admit. "Can't I?"

She shakes her head playfully in reply. Little do either of us know that my chill vibe is about to be turned upside down.

The hostess shows a couple of young guys to a table

near to ours, and all at once, my body shifts gears. On the surface, nothing is out of the ordinary. Yet, my senses tell me another story. I'm flooded with intuitive information, whether I like it or not. The bodily sensations are powerful. Overwhelming.

"Lottie..." I mumble. "It's..."

I grip the arms of my chair tightly, my knuckles turning white. I feel like I might throw up. My psychic abilities are both a blessing and a curse. Mama did her best to train me to handle them. She's the same way. I feel a pang of helplessness, and a part of me wishes Mama was here to offer reassurance that all is well. It doesn't feel like all is well. Nowhere close.

"Basia, breathe," Lottie instructs, finally setting down her phone and leaning towards me. "It's okay. I'm right here."

The glitter inside her plastic phone case catches the light and sparkles in the sun. I nod, beads of perspiration forming on my brow. It's hot outside in the South Florida summer, as usual, but I'm used to that. I work in Hideaway Park in the heat for hours at a time without so much as feeling uncomfortable, as long as there's shade to stand under. This perspiration is different. It comes from nerves. My breathing is shallow, despite Lottie's suggestion.

"I can't..." I begin, my voice shaky.

I shake my head, my long blonde hair moving around my shoulders. I'm tempted to wrap my ample locks around my face and hide underneath them. I begin to trace a plan to cover my eyes completely. Lottie grabs my hand, looking intently at me.

"You can do this," she says, gesturing toward the guys

who caught my attention. "You might be able to help."

She has me there. I do like to help. It seems wrong not to. More than once, I've used my intuition to intervene in situations that would have turned tragic otherwise. I've seen enough evidence to believe that I actually have a gift. Few others can do what I do or see what I see. I feel like I have a responsibility to use the gift I've been given for good. Several of the premonitions I've had have come true recently, and in a very public way. In fact, I'm becoming known around the island for it. I just wish the process of receiving psychic information didn't make my body short circuit. It's exhausting to experience. I also wish it didn't lead people to think I'm a freak.

"I know…" I say. "I know."

Despite my apprehension, I take a deep breath and let it happen. I can't ignore whatever it is these guys need to know. Silently, I give permission to be used as a conduit. As soon as I do, I'm swept away on some kind of wild and crazy ride. It happens fast.

My focus is pulled hard to the young men. I blink a few times as I take in the details. One of them is tall and lanky with pale skin and big teeth. The other is Asian, shorter with tighter features and a muscular build. They appear to be about my age. They're wearing t-shirts, cargo shorts, and flip flops. They're probably tourists, on the island to enjoy the scenery and have a good time. They sort of smile awkwardly as they pass us, but seem uncomfortable. I wonder if they're sensing whatever I am. Lottie looks up, nodding her head at them as the smaller of the two waves politely in return.

Something about these guys strikes me as odd. I don't mean that they're dangerous or anything like that. But the energy surrounding them is palpable. I can't immediately put my finger on it, but it's no accident that their presence has activated my intuition. Or maybe it's my paranoia. I can't be sure which, truth be told. Either way, the hairs on the back of my neck stand on end and a scene flashes before my eyes. It happens involuntarily. I don't want to see it, but I do.

In an instant, what feels like an added layer of vision becomes available to me. I hate it when this happens. *Ugh.* It's terrifying. Within seconds, it's there.

I see the two young guys cowering in the street as ash and debris rain down over them. I see their horrified faces, their cheeks and foreheads stained with soot and blood. They're stumbling, trying to find their footing as they reach out to steady each other. They aren't hurt badly, but they will be if they don't move fast enough. A formidable cloud of dust gathers itself up behind them and barrels their way with a frightening intensity. It threatens to swallow them whole, poisoning their lungs and trapping them within its unrelenting river of death.

"Oh, my God," I say, unable to keep quiet in the face of the horrors I see.

I shake my head harder, as if I might shake free of what's happening.

Lottie notices the expression on my face. She doesn't know what I'm witnessing, but she gets the gist. She knows my intuition is powerful. She's been around me when I've seen things like this before. She's heard my descriptions of the scenes that force themselves into my consciousness. And she's witnessed those very scenes come to pass in the real world, in vivid, living color. She can tell this is serious.

2

MEET

Our waitress shows up balancing a large round tray on her outstretched arm. She's oblivious to my distress, her jet-black curls bouncing against her rich brown skin as she walks. She's perky. Her crisp, white apron is clean. The tag on her breast pocket reads 'Kesha,' the name printed in neat block letters. Kesha looks every bit the part of an island girl, fresh-faced and eager to share the good parts of our little slice of paradise with anyone who has made the trip to spend some time here. She's probably new to Hideaway Isle, her enthusiasm still bubbling over. I'm sure she earns an ample living from tips.

In my experience, tourists are generous. They typically are to me, anyway. I paint portraits of them and read their palms, all right here on the island. It's unpredictable work at times, but I make far more than I would at any regular job. I find that the tourists can tell who is genuinely concerned about them having a good experience. When that sincerity shows through, people relax and let themselves enjoy. Part of that enjoyment is expressed in tips and purchases. After all, they knew they'd spend money when they came here. Even those on the tightest budgets have a little leeway and can choose what to use their cash on.

When I'm working in the park, my goal is to convince the tourists who amble by my station that I'm a good investment. That what I offer is fun, interesting, and useful. In the case of a portrait, their investment pays off in the form of a souvenir they can take home to frame and hang in their home. It's a distinctive souvenir that's far more meaningful than something run-of-the-mill like a flimsy keychain or a coffee mug. While I'm not the best artist to walk this Earth-- or even Hideaway Isle, for that matter-- I'm good. I paint portraits of people's faces, and I pay attention to the subtleties when I do. I take my job seriously. I consider it an honor to have the privilege of recreating the way I see my patrons-- the delight in their eyes as they situate themselves in what they consider to be the most flattering position for me to see them in, the anticipation alive in their expressions while they try not to squirm, and the surprise that ripples throughout their bodies when I present them with the finished product and they see themselves the way I do. It's magical, really.

Some people consider me a street performer instead of a real artist. I disagree with that categorization. Just because my art isn't hanging in some fancy, overpriced gallery in a slick big city doesn't mean I'm not a real artist. I bring beauty into the world through my brush and my paints. And I reflect beauty. The beauty of people. Of the human face. Of the human condition. I won't minimize that. I'm proud of what I can do. Of what I can offer.

Palm reading is different because there isn't anything for my patrons to take home with them as a souvenir. I do the reading, then tell them what I see. There's no recording. They just have to remember. I suppose they could write it down and have the reading framed and hung on the wall. I don't think anyone has ever done that, although I'd never hear about it if they did. When they leave me, they go back to their lives or continue whatever quest they're on. I don't collect their contact information. Maybe I should. But the fleeting nature of the experience doesn't make it any less valuable than a portrait.

When someone comes to me and asks for a reading, they're allowing me a window into the most intimate details of their lives. I never know what kind of information I'll receive intuitively, but I read the lines like Mama taught me until that intangible something takes over. It always happens. I'm *on* when I'm doing it. Like a light switch flipped to allow the electricity to flow through, I let the wisdom in the ether flow through me. When you get right down to it, a palm reading might be even more valuable than a portrait. Maybe the person being read will learn something that will change their lives, or their understanding of themselves. I love it when that happens.

"I have a veggie burger with avocado and slaw," Kesha announces cheerfully, eyeing Lottie.

Kesha obviously remembers who had what, but she's being careful. Confirming things, just to be sure. I'd do the same. Some people who work in hospitality try to make a show of plowing on through without taking a pause to check in with the person they're serving. I prefer a slower, more polite approach, same as Kesha.

"That's mine," Lottie replies, keeping her gaze fixed on me.

Lottie smiles politely as Kesha sets the plate of food down on the table in front of her, but I can see the concern on her face. She's still worried about me and what I've seen related to the young guys nearby. I'm calming down a little now. The initial jolt from the vision has passed through me. It gets easier from here.

Lottie has psychic powers, too. I've been helping her develop her intuition. Her abilities aren't as strong as mine yet, but I suspect that will change in time. She hasn't practiced nearly as much as I have. She has the gift. I can tell. I think she's scared of what it does to me. Of the toll it takes. I don't blame her.

I glance at the guys nearby. They're chatting and laughing. But I can't shake the vision that's still vivid in my mind. It hangs around me, insistent.

"And a burger with bleu cheese," Kesha continues, looking my way. "Fries on the side."

"Hers," Lottie confirms, gesturing towards me.

I nod, my stomach growling as the smell of the food wafts through the air. I haven't eaten yet today. Kesha sets the plate in front of me, the cool porcelain clanking against the metal table. She pulls two rolls of silverware out of her apron and places them in front of each of us. The food looks and smells delicious. The bun is light and fluffy, the burger within looks savory, and the toppings are fresh and crisp.

"Thank you," I say, keeping my head down.

Kesha smiles and tells us to let her know if we need anything at all, then she walks away.

"Can you eat?" Lottie asks. "I'll wait on you, if need be."

I nod.

"I can eat. I'm starving."

I pick up my burger and take a big bite, the flavors bursting in my mouth and satisfying my hunger. Every bit tastes so good. I silently tell my intuition to give me a break while I devour this meal. I need fuel to function, after all. Especially given how much the whole psychic powers thing takes out of me.

Lottie follows my lead, although she eats more slowly. She doesn't pick her phone back up. It's as if she's forgotten all about it and the social media that had her captivated a short time ago. I appreciate that. It's good to know that she'll keep her focus on me when I need her. And I do. I need Lottie. I need her in many ways, not just now, but in general. I hate to admit it, even to myself, but I've become really attached. I look to her to steady me. To support me, emotionally. I do my best to steady and support her, too. I hope the stats are balanced, the give and take fair. No one is keeping score, but I certainly don't want to be a burden. I guess that comes from my upbringing. Mama hated being a burden to the line of men she dated and married. I had a front row seat to that shitshow. I don't want to repeat any of the mistakes my parents made.

"How does it taste?" Lottie asks.

She tears her veggie burger into bite-sized pieces and eats those. She doesn't dig in and get messy like I do. She's naturally more refined.

"Really good," I reply as I wipe the corners of my mouth. "Want a bite?"

I hoist what's left of my juicy burger towards Lottie while I pop a french fry into my mouth with the other hand. As I do, I notice the black bird on the palm frond again. He's still perched there, the palm still swaying gently. Maybe he had gone and returned. Either way, I think he's interested in our food. I wonder if he'll come closer if I set a fry out for him.

"No, thank you," Lottie says. "You know what red meat does to my stomach."

"Suit yourself."

I nod, still looking at the bird as I take my burger back and have another bite. Lottie gets an upset stomach when she eats meat. It's why she consumes mostly vegetarian food. I find it peculiar and have wondered if it's all in her head, but will, of course, support whatever she wants.

"What now?" she asks. "You sure are distractible today."

I point and she follows my gaze to our bird friend.

"I suspect he wants a nibble," I say with a chuckle. "I'm thinking of tossing him a fry or two."

"Don't do it," Kesha jokes, having arrived in time to fill our water glasses and ask how the food is. "If you give him an inch, he'll take a mile."

Her plump lips curl at the edges as she smiles.

"I figured as much," Lottie says. "Birds can be little bitches once they decide to beg."

The three of us laugh together. It feels good and helps me to loosen up. I'm getting full now and my body is calming down. I haven't looked back at the young guys since I started eating. I've sort of put all of that on pause.

I know I'll have to return my attention to them soon, but I'm grateful for the chance to fortify myself first.

"Can I get you anything else?" Kesha asks. "Bird food or otherwise?"

Feeling better, I decide an adult beverage would be nice. Lottie isn't twenty-one yet, but that doesn't mean I can't enjoy myself. She can drive us home. The campground where we stay isn't far from here, anyway.

"You know, Kesha," I begin, "a Leinie would hit the spot. Do you sell them here?"

"A what?" Kesha asks.

"A Leinenkugel," I say. "It's a Wisconsin thing. Best beer I've ever tasted. Brewed in Chippewa Falls."

"I don't think we have that," she replies. "Sorry."

I shrug. "It was worth a shot. How about a strawberry daiquiri? Can you make me one of those?"

"The bartender certainly can," she replies. "I'll be right back."

Lottie lowers her brows and eyes me skeptically, though a playful smile tells me she doesn't object.

"It's a little early for alcohol, isn't it? You know how you get."

I know exactly how I get when I drink-- horny as hell. Lottie knows, too, which is why she mentioned it.

"Nonsense," I say with a sly smile. "It's never early enough. We have the afternoon to ourselves. Maybe a nap should be on the agenda. I'm not going to work in the park until around four."

Tourists typically gather in Hideaway Park to watch the sunset on the water. It doesn't tend to get crowded until evening. I've experimented with going earlier in the day but have never earned enough to make it worth the time. It's best to enjoy my day, then work in the evening. I'm happier with more time off, and I maximize the hours I spend.

"A nap, huh?" Lottie teases. "Just a nap? Should I hold you to that?"

"Babe, you can hold me to anything you like," I reply.

I wink and we chuckle as we finish our meals. When my burger is gone, I pick at my fries. I toss a couple onto the ground below the little bird. He doesn't hesitate, diving greedily and scarfing them down. I follow up with a handful, and he eats those, too. By the time the fries are all gone, Kesha brings my daiquiri. I sip it slowly, letting the fruity flavor move across my tongue as the cool slush slides down my throat. I remove the whole strawberry from the side of the glass and bite into it. The juice runs down my chin. Lottie leans forward and wipes it gently with her napkin, her eyes meeting mine. She's thinking about making love. I can tell.

"Ah, that hits the spot," I say. "Maybe Jimmy Buffet should change the song to *Cheeseburger and Daiquiri in Paradise*."

She tosses the napkin at me playfully.

"You're so silly," she says.

"Don't you mean so much fun?"

She shakes her head and laughs. I continue to nurse my drink, enjoying every sip. I know it's nearly time. I must address the young guys before I can leave here and go about the rest of my day. Lottie knows it, too. She glances in their direction. Her expression turns to one of surprise when she lays eyes on them.

"Oh," she mumbles.

"What is it?" I ask, turning my head in their direction.

The tall guy with the teeth is coming towards us. He's nearly at our table. There's no time to hide or make an escape. Looks like I'm stuck talking to him, whether I like it or not. Good thing I'm fed and loosened up.

"Hey, this will sound crazy, but I have to ask. Are you Basia Guthrie?" he says as he comes to a stop next to me. "From Fox, Wisconsin?"

A jolt moves through me and my body stiffens. He's right. But how? I haven't even told Lottie the name of the city where I'm from.

3

WALK A MILE

There's a lot Lottie doesn't know or understand about me. An awful lot. It's my fault, mostly. There's plenty I haven't told her. I'm too ashamed. I hate being ashamed, with every fiber of my being. I'd prefer to be one of those resilient types who doesn't let prior traumas change them. I'd like to rise above, and all that bullshit. Yet, I can't help it. I'm deeply, heart wrenchingly ashamed. Like a wounded animal, hobbling around on a bum leg and pretending nothing is wrong so a predator doesn't make an afternoon snack out of me.

Sometimes, I worry the differences between us are too great, the chasm that separates us too vast. And I have good reasons for worrying.

First of all, I don't come from a nice family like Lottie does. Sure, she has experienced more than her share of loss. Her dad was killed in a boating accident when she was a baby. Then her mom was killed in a bicycle accident right in front of Lottie's innocent, twelve-year-old eyes. After that horrific event, Lottie's sister, Margot,

got the hell out of dodge and joined the Navy, leaving Lottie with no one to look after her but her elderly grandpa. A handful of other relatives also died young, or so Lottie thought.

That's tough, certainly. But it's nowhere near as tough as living with people who couldn't care less what happened to you. That was my sad story. My dismal existence.

"Who's asking?" I reply to the gangly young man who stands waiting.

He's gawking at me like I'm a circus animal. He's looking at Lottie, too, apparently sizing her up and assessing the relationship between us. I don't mean to be rude, but I'm about to be. I have little patience for this shit.

He raises a hand over his eyes to block the sun and get a better look.

"You don't remember?" he asks, his tone changing. "Fox Senior High. Mrs. McClanahan's history class?"

I wrack my brain. That's the name of my high school, alright. And I was, in fact, in Mrs. McClanahan's history class. Second period. But I don't remember this guy. *Should I?*

Lottie eyes me, interested in the new information. She's always wanted to learn more about my past. I've done my damnedest to keep her from finding out much. It's not that I don't trust her. I do. It's just-- like I said-- I'm ashamed.

My childhood wasn't pleasant. I wasn't *wanted*. Not really. Mama was too busy trying to please a man to pay much attention to me. And the men, well, they just wanted me out of their sight. I was nothing more than a complication they'd rather not deal with. Every one of them was the overbearing, controlling type who got rough with Mama if she didn't do exactly what they wanted. She married four of them after Pa left. She was on marriage number five when I last spoke to her. I wouldn't be surprised if she was up to six or seven by now.

I'm smart enough to know that the odds of staying married go down with each failed attempt. I don't think Mama stands a chance in hell of having a happy marriage at this point. They're bad guys, for the most part, but she's the common denominator. She chose them. Something is seriously wrong with her decision-making abilities. As long as she wants that kind of riffraff, she'll attract it. Some sleazeball will show up and play house every time she's in the market for a new one. There doesn't seem to be a shortage of sleazeballs, unfortunately.

I'd prefer to leave all of that behind me. The fact that I've come so far only to run into a guy who recognizes me from high school seems like a cruel twist of fate. Don't I deserve a clean slate? A place where no one recognizes me as poor, pitiful Basia Guthrie?

Maybe it's time to change my name. Maybe I should have done so a long time ago. At minimum, I could use a different last name. I feel more connected to Basia since it's what people call me, but Guthrie seems like nothing more than unnecessary baggage. Maybe someday, Lottie and I will get married, and I'll change my name to Basia Callaway. Her family is decent. Noble, even. I think a lot of her sister, Margot. I have great respect for her career in the Navy. Although, if Margot marries Rags, she might go and change her last name to Bertram.

I take a breath before answering the guy who activated my intuition. I must remain mindful of what I saw. The ash and threatening cloud of dust looms. I get the distinct sense that the scene I envisioned has yet to happen. It's in his future. Or, at least, it will be if I don't say or do anything to stop it.

"Should I know you?" I ask, hoping to buy myself more time before I have to offer any information.

I don't deny that he correctly named my high school and history teacher, although I considered it. It would have been easy enough to claim I didn't know what he was talking about. That is, unless he'd pulled up yearbook photos online or something. He seems insistent, like the damn little bird. I wouldn't put anything past him at this point.

I'm afraid. No one from home knows I'm gay. I don't want them to. Not yet, anyway. I'm not prepared for that. They could tell Mama, and I'm not sure she could handle it. She's always seemed frail, like something could take her down if it was too upsetting. I don't want to be the reason she's pushed over the edge. And poor Lottie doesn't realize the stakes.

"So, it really is you, Basia?" the guy says, glancing at his friend and giving him a thumbs up.

They're probably on vacation and going back to Wisconsin soon. That means they'll be able to spread the word around town about what they learned here. It's a small town. Word travels fast.

I exhale a breath I've been holding as the smoky scene forces its way back into my consciousness. I decide that I have no choice but to fess up and let this situation unfold as it may. Lottie was right about me wanting to help. I truly do. And that requires that I remain open and willing to be of service.

Dammit.

"Yes, I'm Basia," I confirm. "I attended Fox Senior High School in Wisconsin. And you're right, I was in Mrs. McClanahan's class. But I'm sorry, I don't think I remember you."

He grins from ear to ear.

"I'm Nigel. Remember? I sat in the back row and slept every chance I could get. Until Mrs. McC busted my balls and gave me detention. She did that a lot."

"Nigel…" I mutter, scanning my memory.

The name is vaguely familiar. And I do recall a trio of jocks who slept in the back of history class.

"Nigel Tate," he offers. "Junior."

"Ah," I say as it comes flooding back to me. The Junior did it. "Now I remember."

Nigel Tate Jr. was a pretty-boy jock whose daddy somehow got him out of every bit of trouble he got himself into… and he got himself into a lot. He's understating things when he mentions sleeping in the back row. I'm not sure how he passed the class-- any class, for that matter. Nigel was completely disinterested in his own education. I suspect he would have been expelled from the school if it weren't for Nigel Sr. intervening. I don't know how the elder Nigel made his kid's trouble disappear like he did. But maybe that falls into the category of things I'll never truly understand. I never had a dad interested enough to stay in my life, let alone try to get me out of trouble. Who am I to speculate on such matters?

"Wow!" Lottie exclaims. She scoots forward in her

chair, the excitement beaming from her face. "What are the odds, Basia? Who could guess that you'd run into an old friend from Wisconsin all the way down here on Hideaway Isle?"

Nigel's eye twitches and his shoulders seem to tighten.

"I'm not sure I'd call us friends, exactly…" he mumbles, balling one hand up into a fist at his side.

"More like acquaintances," I add.

Nigel was pretty horrible to me. Once, he pinned me against a wall below the bleachers in the football stadium and put his hand up my shirt. When I resisted his advances, he shoved me so hard I hit the back of my head hard on the concrete behind me. I had a headache for nearly a week after that. And the physical pain was nothing compared to the emotional pain of being teased by Nigel and his fellow cronies. He was deeply insulted that I wasn't interested in him. His fragile ego couldn't take it.

Anxiety crawls up my neck and makes my face flush. Nigel was one of the popular kids in school. I'm not sure what he would have against me in particular as compared to any other classmate, but something he remembers seems to irritate him.

"Are you two… *together*?" he asks, out of the blue.

I know exactly what he means. Of course, I do. He probably saw Lottie and me holding hands. Or maybe he heard us talking about our plans for an afternoon nap. I suddenly want to crawl under the table and disappear. Running away would do the trick, too. My fight or flight response is leaning heavily towards flight. This is exactly what I've dreaded since the moment he used my name.

Lottie smiles proudly. She's used to being open about

her sexuality. Here in South Florida, it isn't usually an issue. People are mostly accepting. Gay and lesbian couples are everywhere. Lottie doesn't understand what it's like to live in a place where being gay could get you beaten up. Or worse.

"We are," Lottie confirms before I can intervene. "Our one-year anniversary is coming up next month. She's the best girlfriend ever."

My pulse quickens. I know what's coming. Nigel stands silently for a moment, then bursts out laughing. His tone is mocking. Lottie doesn't realize it yet, but he's making fun of me. Just like he did in school.

"Well, that explains a lot," he says. "Basia the lesbo... No wonder."

His voice is sour. Uncaring. I feel violated just hearing it. It scrapes through my ears like sandpaper. *How dare he?* I want to speak up. To defend myself. To defend Lottie. But my voice fails me.

"What are you even talking about?" Lottie asks.

She isn't angry yet, but she will be when she fully realizes what's happening. She's feisty. Her voice won't fail her when it comes time for her to use it. Nigel continues to laugh, one hand on his belly for dramatic effect. His friend watches us but doesn't get up to join us. Or to intervene.

"I'm talking about Basia being queer," he chides. "A dyke. I knew she was weird, but I didn't realize she was a carpet muncher! This explains everything."

Lottie's face falls slack as she listens, the pride washed away.

"Wait until I tell the boys back home," Nigel continues. "They're going to die when they find out.

Especially Tom Patroski. He tried desperately to get Basia into bed and took it as a personal failure that he couldn't. I guess he's off the hook now."

I shake my head. My entire body breaks out into a cold sweat.

"Nigel, please," I say. "My parents don't know. I'd… I'd like to keep this private."

His laughter sounds like that of an evil movie villain.

"Are you kidding me?" he asks. "The people at home deserve to hear the truth. You can't go around teasing guys without having the decency to tell them why you won't see things through. It's cruel and unusual. Nobody likes a tease."

"And Basia deserves her privacy," Lottie says insistently, sitting up straight in her seat. "If you know what's good for you, you'll respect her wishes and back the fuck off."

Nigel turns to face her. His expression is flat. He can hardly fathom a girl like her standing up to him. His fragile ego is rearing its ugly head again.

"What did you say to me?" he asks, spittle forming at the corners of his mouth.

Lottie stands, the chair toppling behind her.

"You heard me," she replies.

And with that, a hush falls over the crowd on the patio as they watch and wait.

It must look strange to see little, petite Lottie taking on a tall guy like Nigel. She's scrappy, but he has nearly a foot on her. No one watching can predict what's going to happen next, but whatever it is, they don't want to miss it.

4

STANDING

"Little girl," Nigel says through gritted teeth, "you had better be real careful about what comes out of your mouth next."

"Or what?"

She's brave, I'll give her that. I'm still frozen, unable to say or do anything helpful. My mouth hangs open in awe of Lottie's courage.

Kesha walks out from the kitchen at a normal pace, then slows as she must realize that something unusual is going on. It's impossible to miss the silence and the captivated crowd, but she's confused. She glances at me as if I'll explain. Even if I could find words, I'm not sure where to begin. My past, present, and future are whirling around me in a blur. My insecurities are on full display for everyone here to see. It's excruciating. I'm embarrassed that Kesha has to witness this.

"Or I'll teach you a lesson," Nigel grunts as he cracks his knuckles. "Right here in front of everyone."

Lottie scoffs in reply. "You wouldn't hit a girl, would you? Didn't your daddy teach you better than that?"

"I'd hit a dyke..."

A collective groan sounds from the crowd. This has crossed into harassment, no doubt. Nigel is treating us poorly because we're lesbians. And if he lays hands on Lottie, it might even be considered a hate crime. Plenty of onlookers are here to witness his actions.

Despite my anger towards Nigel Jr., I can't shake the ominous, fiery scene and the feeling that I must warn him about it. I want to be better than Nigel. I don't mean that in a competitive or immature way. But I want to be true to who I am, rather than stoop to his level of pettiness. The person I am today has been hard earned. I don't intend to lose ground.

"Disgusting," Lottie shouts. "But I'm not scared of you. I've faced worse. And besides, I'll bet you're all talk and no action."

Lottie's right. She has faced worse. I saw it with my own eyes.

When the madman held us captive recently, Lottie experienced the brunt of the trauma. She was tied to a chair while several hired guns tossed Rags' house. When they wanted her to talk, they threatened to take off one of her fingers with a cigar cutter. She was terrified. She screamed. A lot. I snuck out an upstairs window onto the roof and eventually made my way off the property to get help. I hated to leave Lottie, but I had to. I heard her cries yet had to remain silent and hidden. I didn't know if she'd be alive by the time I returned, but she was. And it changed her. She found strength she didn't know she had. Nigel is a light-weight threat compared to all of that.

It's interesting. Of the two of us, I was the stronger one that day. I held myself together as Lottie fell apart. It was Margot and Rags who saved us. I can't compete with Navy training like they've both had, though I did my part and my best. But today, in the here and now, I'm the one coming undone. Nigel is touching on my childhood hurts and causing all kinds of negative emotional stuff to surface. It's as if I'm Superman-- or woman-- and he's brought kryptonite to render me weak and useless.

Come to think of it, Superman is another one of the things I remember Pa liking along with Jimmy Buffet. He approved of Henry Cavill in the superhero role, but always said he preferred the original Superman movies starring Christopher Reeve. I'm not positive I have this right, but I think Pa watched Christopher Reeve when he was a kid. The memory is jarring. I haven't thought about Pa and Superman for a long time. Maybe the stress I'm currently under is loosening things up in my brain, allowing access to memories that had been buried. Pa's love for the Green Bay Packers comes to mind, too. And his preference for peanut butter and banana sandwiches as a late-night snack. Maybe there's a bigger reason for what I'm going through. Or maybe I'm trying desperately to put a good spin on what's quickly turning into a no good, horrible day. I admit that I sometimes try too hard to look on the bright side. A bright side doesn't always exist.

Suddenly, Nigel lunges toward Lottie, knocking into our table with his thighs and sending plates, glasses, and silverware crashing to the ground. The shattering sound reverberates throughout the area. I wince, my entire body tight as a drum in anticipation of what's to come. Nigel stops just short of Lottie, his hand outstretched as if he'll slap her. It's impossible to tell that he'll stop short, for sure, until the very last second. To everyone's surprise, Lottie doesn't flinch. The crowd gasps. She crosses her arms over her chest and narrows her eyes. I'm so proud of my girl.

"Is that all you've got?" Lottie asks.

"Why, I oughta..." Nigel purses his lips and clenches both hands into tight fists.

His friend has remained quiet at their table until now, but the guy looks like he's had about enough. He shifts his gaze down and shakes his head. I can't tell if he wants to pull Nigel off of Lottie or provide him reinforcement. Surely, the guy doesn't want to pile on under these conditions. Most decent people would put an end to this and drag their miserable friend away. Although, since he's a friend of Nigel's, who knows?

Lottie takes a step closer, egging Nigel on. At this point, I fear she's in over her head. When does bravery become foolishness? I suspect we're nearly there. Kesha sighs heavily behind me, and it seems like she's deciding whether or not to intervene. I think we all hope that Nigel will sit down and leave it-- leave *us*-- alone. Lottie and I aren't looking for a fight. In fact, I'd like nothing more than to rewind to about an hour ago so we could eat lunch somewhere else and avoid this whole mess.

"Stop!" I say, standing. "Stop it, right now. I can't let this go on any longer."

"Sit down, Basia," Nigel says. "You're too meek for this. Let your attack dyke handle things. That is what you have her for, isn't it? Though it might have been better if you'd chosen someone who looks more butch."

I shudder under his verbal attack. His words sting. I despise this part of being gay. Straight people don't get harassed about their most personal relationships. Their choices in a romantic partner aren't scrutinized like this. It's ridiculously unfair. I'm sick of hearing about the gay agenda, as if we're trying to take over and make the world a terrible place. I've got news for the haters-- the gay agenda is as mundane as they can possibly imagine. You know, things like making breakfast, walking the dog, and maybe going for a swim in the evening before dinner. We're human beings, no different than any others. We love our friends and families. We just want to be left alone to live normal lives in peace.

Nigel continues, fed by my pain and suffering. He smells fear and it's making him even more viscous.

"Let me see if I can sum this up," he says loudly, placing a hand on his chin and squinting as if he's about to spout wisdom that the crowd will benefit from. "You couldn't protect your slutty mama from all those lowlife men who abused her, Basia Guthrie, so you thought you'd get a woman of your own who you'd treat better… far, far away from home where no one knows you. You'd wine and dine her with a few scraps of money you managed to make, you'd get into her pants, and then the two of you would pretend to be a real couple. Only, you're too much of a scared little girl to actually do right by your woman. You can't protect her any more than you could protect Mama Guthrie… or was it Matthews, or Dickerson, or Pike, or Rawlins… hell, I've lost count, haven't you?" He's on a roll and doesn't want to quit until I'm thoroughly humiliated. "Does your mama keep the welcome mat at the foot of her bed… or am I mistaken about how that works?"

This time, Lottie lunges Nigel's way. She reaches him in a flash, her right arm poised to deliver an uppercut to his jaw. I leap in between them and grab Lottie at the waist. I'm a little taller, but it takes all of my strength to move her. I lift her feet off the ground and swing us around so that my back is to Nigel just as he lands a blow that falls hard on my head. I stumble, reeling. Lottie and I tumble to the ground, knocking chairs down with us. The crowd groans and I hear movement. I'm too dazed to focus on anything, but I get the feeling that the onlookers have been spurred into action.

I've heard about how a crowd can be the worst place to look for help. There's a term for the effect. I remember learning it in a psychology class in high school but can't recall what it's called right now. The basic premise is that, in a crowd, people tend to assume that someone else will help, so they don't take action. In contrast, if just one or two people witness a situation where help is needed, they're more likely to jump in and assist because they think no one else is there to do it. They perceive the responsibility as being squarely on their shoulders. It's fascinating, really. Human psychology is fascinating. I enjoyed the intro class that I took. Maybe I should go back to school and study psychology. Maybe I could somehow work to change negative attitudes and stereotypes.

I find myself mumbling under my breath as I try to regain my bearings. "The bystander effect," I say to no one in particular. "That's what it's called… But we need help..."

Lottie squirms in my arms. She doesn't say anything right away, but I know she wants to get up and go after Nigel again. She's irritated that I stopped her. I keep a tight hold. She tries to wriggle free. We're both on the concrete, our limbs twisted unnaturally due to the way we landed. My head spins as table legs, toppled chairs, and broken dinnerware come into view. I don't see blood, but I smell it. I think I might be bleeding.

"Let me go, Basia!" Lottie shouts. "I mean it."

I shake my head. I don't know where Nigel is. He might hit me again. I won't let him hit Lottie. I hear more shuffling and a commotion amongst the crowd, but I still can't make sense of what they're doing. Maybe someone is keeping Nigel away from us. Then I hear a familiar voice.

"Lottie, we're here. Tell me what you need."

It's Margot. I squint and her face comes into view. She's crouched in front of us, wearing one of her Navy t-shirts that I've come to realize is her usual. This one is dark blue with white letters. Her brown hair is pulled back and tucked into a neat ponytail. She looks kind of like an angel. I think that's because I'm hurt and scared. And I'm not used to having people in my life who show up and help me. Tears spring to my eyes. I'm touched.

"Margot?" Lottie asks, surprised. She's not quite used to having people show up for her either.

"Yes," Margot confirms. "Rags is here, too." She gestures behind us, and I get the idea that he's dealing with Nigel.

Thank God.

"Here," Rags calls from somewhere in the distance. "This little pissant won't be bothering you anymore."

I hear Nigel groan. Some other voices rise, too. They must be helping Rags. Not that he needs it. He's a former Navy SEAL. Rags keeps that information quiet around here, but he and Margot told Lottie and me. The guy is huge, in fantastic shape, and he's trained by the U.S. military as an elite fighter. He's tough. A good one to have in our corner.

"Oh, Basia," Margot says, focusing her attention on me. "You're bleeding."

"Am I?" I ask, raising a hand to the back of my head. I feel dampness.

"I'll call 9-1-1!" Kesha announces. She hurries inside and disappears behind the restaurant door.

I blink slowly. Something is wrong. Something is… changing. My consciousness is slipping like a manual transmission with stripped gears. I can't seem to stay awake.

"Basia, stay with me," Margot urges.

Lottie gets loose and positions herself above me. "Basia, you're scaring me. Please, stay awake."

Someone has wadded up a cloth napkin and stuffed ice inside. Margot puts it on the back of my head. I feel the shock of the cold against my skin.

"I…" I begin, fumbling for words. "I need to tell him what's going to happen. The fire. And the dust. It's some kind of explosion. I saw it so clearly. Nigel and his friend were there, covered in blood and ash… And then the dust cloud came and swallowed them. They'll die if I don't warn them…"

I hear a collective gasp from around me. I can't be sure that what I'm seeing is right, but I think I spot mobile phone cameras pointing in my direction.

"Are they filming me?" I ask. "Why are they doing that?"

Before Lottie or Margot can answer, I lose my grip on waking consciousness. Everything goes black.

5

MAMAS

Is it just me, or does everyone want their mama when they're sick or injured? No matter how sour the relationship is or how many miles apart we may be, I find myself wishing for Mama's presence in times like these.

I remember being a little girl and her tending to me when I was sick. I never came down with anything very serious-- just typical childhood colds and flus-- but Mama took extra good care of me when I was under the weather. She'd prop me up on the couch with pillows and blankets so I could watch TV while resting. Our only TV at that time was in the living room, and taking the prime, coveted spot on the couch was a special privilege that I wasn't usually allowed. Mama would take great care to make sure I was warm and comfortable, putting thick socks on my feet and tucking the blankets high under my chin. When I was all warm and cozy, she'd retreat to the kitchen and make me soup.

Mama didn't cook all that often, but when I was sick, she made from scratch. Sometimes, she even made it with dumplings. When it was ready, she'd bring it to me in the living room-- another special privilege-- so I could sip the broth and nibble small bites without upsetting my sick stomach or hurting my sore throat. When I could handle it, she'd add homemade chili or macaroni and cheese to the mix. There's a good reason those dishes are known as comfort foods. Their warm, tasty goodness sure hits the spot when you're feeling puny.

Once, in second grade, I broke my arm when I fell off the monkey bars at the school playground. I'd been hanging upside down by my bent legs and trying to adjust positions by climbing onto the top of the metal structure. I'd done it hundreds of times, yet somehow, I missed a bar during the maneuver and went crashing to the ground with my outstretched arm below me. It was a pretty nasty injury. My elbow took the brunt of the impact and ended up visibly out of place. I think I freaked my classmates out. Several of them ran screaming when they saw my mangled limb.

This is probably messed up, but despite the pain in my arm and the apprehension about what would happen at the emergency room, I was happy to be injured. I know. Messed up, right? I was happy because I knew Mama would take extra special care of me while I recovered. I was desperate for her time and attention.

Pa was gone by then, and Mama was on marriage number two, to Carl Matthews. Carl didn't have kids of his own and made it known that he didn't want any. He didn't care for me much either. I tried to make friends with him, but the only acknowledgement of my existence came in the form of him telling Mama to get rid of me. She'd shuttle me anywhere she could to keep me out of Carl's way-- to friends' houses for sleepovers, to my Aunt Portia's place, and even to some of my teachers' houses in a pinch. Portia is Pa's sister. She continued to be nice to Mama and me after he left. She's the one I stayed with most. At least, she was family and made me feel like I had a right to be there. But she wasn't always available. She's a nurse who worked long shifts, so she couldn't keep me every time Mama asked. Spending the night with teachers was the most embarrassing of all. I can still feel the cold sweat on my palms and the butterflies in my stomach that showed up each time I had to face that uncomfortable situation. Mama had some nerve, asking them if I could spend the night. I'd cringe when they'd say yes and then she'd add instructions about how they should make sure I washed my hair. I was mortified.

When I broke my arm, I knew I'd be allowed to stay home, whether Carl liked it or not. Mama might have been cowardly when it came to standing up for me in our regular, daily lives, but she had certain limits. I knew she wouldn't push me away when I had a broken bone. See, there was a time after Pa left and before Carl came into our lives when it was just Mama and me. She was attentive then, like a mother should be. I knew that my injury would put me on a fast track to getting that Mama back, even if only for a few days. And I was right. She parked me on the couch and tended to me with the most loving care. When Carl complained, she told him to shove it. Surprisingly, he allowed her to care for me and didn't get in the way. Not for a while, anyway.

I haven't seen Mama in a long time, but if she could somehow show up here on Hideaway Isle and make a batch of that tasty chicken soup, it would be everything to me.

As I begin to wake up, I think she's in the room. I feel a presence near my right shoulder.

"Mama?" I ask expectantly. "Is that you?"

"Hello, dear," a warm female voice says. "How are you feeling?"

It isn't her. The disappointment oozes out of me and spreads throughout the room like thick fog. I realize it sounds silly, but I wish it was her. For some strange reason, she's all I can think about.

A graying African American woman with pretty braids in her hair and a warm smile comes into view. She's wearing scrubs. A rectangular badge featuring her picture dangles from a clip on her shirt pocket. I think she's a nurse, like Aunt Portia.

"Sorry," I say. "I thought you were my mom."

She pats my arm gently, then gives it a squeeze. Her presence is comforting. I see why she's a nurse. I'll bet she's a good one.

"I'm Agnes," she says. "Agnes Swanson. Your nurse. I'm here to take care of you. You received a blow to the head. Do you remember?"

She lifts one arm and stares at a wristwatch when I don't answer. It takes me a minute to figure out what she's doing, but I finally realize that she's checking my pulse.

"Don't you have machines for that?" I ask. I'm irritable. I probably sound curt, even though I don't mean to. My head is killing me.

Agnes chuckles. "Nothing wrong with doing things the old-fashioned way when it works."

"Am I in the hospital?"

She nods, patting my arm again. Tears form in my eyes. I try to keep them at bay, but they flow freely, wetting my cheeks. I look down at the blanket that covers me and am reminded of how Mama used to cover me up when I was hurt. I struggle to hold myself together. I've pretended to be fine without her. I didn't have a choice. But I'm *not* fine without her. Not even close.

"You want your mom, don't you?" she asks, giving me a sympathetic smile.

I'm too choked up to speak, but I nod back. I wonder what's wrong with me. I'm not usually this emotional. If Mama could just be here somehow, I'd be so glad. I want to see her walk through the door, her familiar face fraught with worry and concern for me, her only child. In my best-case scenario, she'd rush over and hug me. She'd wipe the tears from my cheeks, and she'd stroke my hair like she used to when I was little. I'd give anything to have that happen. *Anything.* It feels like I'm a million miles away from home. I review in my mind the reasons I left Fox, Wisconsin and came all the way to Hideaway Isle, but none of them seem good enough now. At least, they aren't good enough reasons to have cut contact completely. I could kick myself for walking away like I did.

"I understand," Agnes says. "Lots of us want our moms when we're hurt. I know I do. And my babies are grown, but they still call me to take care of them when they're sick. I think that's just the way it works. It's human nature."

I try to smile. I manage a small one in between sniffles.

"You're not alone," she continues. "I'm here. And

your friends are in the waiting room. Once the doctor checks you out and says it's okay, they'll be able to come back and be with you. Well, two at a time, anyway. I hear there's a slew of them out there."

I had forgotten all about Lottie, Margot, and Rags. I guess I was too preoccupied with my thoughts about Mama. I feel silly. Maybe it's due to medicine they gave me… if they gave me any. I don't know for sure. But a slew? That sounds like more than just the three of them. I wonder who else is here. Who else would show up for me? I'm a loner. I don't have many friends.

"Okay," I say. "Good. And thank you. You're very nice."

"You're very welcome, my dear."

Agnes lifts a clipboard from a slot at the bottom of my bed, then glances at the machines nearby. She scribbles some notes down. She's recording my vitals in my chart. It occurs to me later than it should. My thinking is slower than usual. I'm sluggish and confused. I don't like it.

"Do you remember what happened?" she asks, trying again.

I shake my head quickly, without trying to recall the injury. It's in my memory somewhere. I can tell. But it feels buried deep, in a place I can't quite reach. Or maybe a place I don't want to. Agnes makes a note of my response. She doesn't seem upset with me. I'll bet she's a good mama. The thought sends tears streaming down my cheeks again. I'm such a blubbering mess. *Ugh.*

"Hey, now," Agnes says as she walks back around to my side and takes both of my hands in her own. "Everything is okay, Miss Basia. You're going to get through this. I promise. It feels hard now, but you'll take one step at a time until you reach better days."

"Yeah," I mumble. "Okay."

I try to look on the bright side. Truly, I do. It's what keeps me adaptable and resilient. If it weren't for my positive outlook, I'd probably be living a miserable life right now. More miserable than this one. Even though I have emotional hurts and I'm laying in a hospital bed with physical hurts now, too, my life is fairly good. I've made the best of a difficult childhood. I'll continue to see the glass as half full. It's the only way.

Agnes doesn't know me. I'm sure she doesn't realize how strong I really am. She's seeing me at my worst. My most vulnerable.

"Believe you me," she implores, squeezing my hands. "I want a more convincing reply. You hear me?"

"Okay," I say, louder this time. I reach deep and pull strength from my reserves. "I believe you. I'll do it."

Agnes tilts her head back and closes her eyes. She reminds me of the ladies I knew at a church we used to attend when I was a kid-- a spirit as strong as the day is long. "Tell it to me, Basia," she says. "I want you to say it loud and proud. There will be better days for you ahead."

I smile and squeeze her hands back, then I sit up as straight as I can and puff my chest out. I'm wobbly and sore, but I feel the certainty rise in me.

"There will be better days ahead. I know there will," I state resolutely. And I mean it.

Satisfied, Agnes says goodbye and leaves the room, promising to send the doctor as soon as possible so he can clear me for visitors. She tells me to rest but encourages me to wait a while longer before turning on the TV or accessing the internet on my mobile phone. I find her request strange but agree to do as she says. I'm not quite myself right now anyway. A little nap would probably do me good.

When Agnes leaves the room and the door closes behind her, I shut my eyes and drift off to sleep, snug and cared for in the blankets she tucked so lovingly around me. I still wish Mama was here, but Agnes went a long way toward filling her shoes. Right now, I'll take every bit of mothering I can get.

6

GUESSWORK

I can't tell how long I sleep, but it seems like just a few minutes after I closed my eyes that a young Indian doctor in a white coat walks in without so much as knocking on the door. He shuffles his feet and holds his arms awkwardly at his sides. Maybe I'm imagining things, but he seems nervous. I hope he knows what he's doing. I've never been in the hospital before, only the emergency room once, so I don't know what to expect.

"Hello, there, Miss Guthrie," he says, shoving a hand towards me.

I reach out to shake it. His touch is soft. Kind, even. It puts me at ease. As I stare up at his coal-black beard and silky hair, I'm struck by how handsome he is. His eyes are intelligent, although they don't meet mine for long.

"Hi," I reply.

"I'm Dr. Yash Khatri," he adds.

He seems to be forcing himself to make eye contact. I nod. I must look confused because he tells me I can call him Dr. K if his full name is too much of a mouthful.

"Oh, that's okay," I say. "I want to call you your full name. Dr. Khatri, right? My mind isn't quite back to normal, but I can remember your name. It's important."

He opens his eyes wide and smiles approvingly. His body language shifts as he relaxes. "Wow," he says. "You're quite a remarkable young woman. I can tell this already. What you said is different from the answers I usually hear."

"Really?" I ask. "That's kind of surprising."

Dr. Khatri reminds me of a chemistry teacher I had during my sophomore year of high school. They're both quiet and smart, with an air of wisdom hiding behind their cool exteriors. I believe I'm in good hands with the doctor. I trust him to take good care of me.

"Really," he confirms. "People don't usually want to learn something new and unfamiliar, especially when they're in the hospital and worried about their health. The fact that you are willing to stretch to show me respect says a whole lot about you."

I shrug. "Well, then, good. I guess. I do respect you."

The doc stares at me a moment, apparently lost in thought about his name. I'm glad I can offer him a small dose of the comfort he and Agnes are providing me. We're a good team. Finally, he snaps out of it, removing a stethoscope from around his neck and moving to listen to my lungs. The circular metal is cold against my back.

"Deep breath," he instructs.

I do as he asks, breathing in and out several times as he listens to different places along the core of me. The silence makes me feel like I should say something to break it, but I realize Dr. Khatri needs it quiet to hear my heart and lungs. When he's finished with that part of the examination, he returns the stethoscope to his neck and pokes around the glands in my throat. He smiles politely and lowers one brow as he thinks, presumably about what he's feeling in my neck. This all seems overkill for a head injury, but I haven't been to that many doctors in my life. I'm no expert.

"Is everything okay?" I ask, unable to keep quiet any longer.

Dr. Khatri purses his lips and looks at the floor. I repeat my question when he doesn't respond right away.

"Doctor, is something wrong?"

He sighs heavily and wads up his face.

Why do I get the feeling there was more to Agnes' pep talk than meets the eye? It sounded like she was referring to my head injury and the related hospital stay, but I'm not sure that's all she was getting at. If something is seriously wrong with me, I'm not sure what I'll do. My mind spins as I consider the scary possibilities.

I don't have health insurance. It's been on my to-do list-- you know, to get a real job that provides insurance and paid time off. Like a bonafide grown up. I admit it hasn't been a priority though. I'm young and healthy. At least, I *was* before Nigel became violent. Health insurance was one of those things that didn't seem pressing. Now I wish I'd given more of my attention to such matters. I'm not sure how I'll be able to pay for this hospital stay, let alone any others that might be coming down the pike. Do hospitals like this one turn people away if they can't pay? My comfortable living from tips won't be so comfortable under the strain of medical bills. And besides those frightening logistics, I don't want to be sick.

Us Guthries come from a long line of healthy stock

and so I haven't seen any family members severely ill, but I watched a neighbor back in Fox whittle away to nothing and then die of breast cancer. It was horrible for poor old Linda Watson. I call her old because she was old compared to me, but I don't think she was any more than fifty. I know that isn't old. Not really. It's too young to die. Things intensified when the cancer moved to her liver. She suffered terrible pain and discomfort, especially near the end. At one point, doctors said it was in her bones, her lungs, her brain, and even in the fluid around her heart. She was eaten up with it. She didn't stand a chance. I was in fifth grade then, and I remember hearing Linda's cries when I brought her mail from the box at the street and placed it in the slot at her front door. I guess I was quiet enough to sneak up on Linda because she yelled like she didn't know I was there. I still have bad dreams about it every now and then.

Maybe that's one reason I'm uncomfortable with silence. If I keep talking and make my presence known, maybe I won't find out any harsh realities I'm not ready to face. I'll bet that's it. The human mind is a curious thing.

After a few excruciating minutes, Dr. Khatri reaches out and gives my shoulder a gentle squeeze. He can probably tell I'm worried.

"No, nothing like that," he says. "Nothing is wrong with you. You're okay. You're *going* to be okay--physically."

I exhale a breath I didn't realize I'd been holding.

"Good," I mumble.

"We need to keep a close eye on you, though. Head injuries can be tricky."

I nod. "Then what is it? Something is bothering you, right?"

After the way I grew up, I've become good at reading faces and body language. No way in hell will the doc convince me that nothing else is going on. There's something he wants to say-- or ask. He's holding back. Although, I admit I'm still groggy and out of sorts. I suppose the meds might be making me more touchy than usual.

He pulls his hand away from my shoulder and sits down on a stool beside my bed. I eye him nervously and suddenly wish Lottie was with me. Getting Mama here might be impossible but fetching my girlfriend from the waiting room should be easy enough.

"I…" Dr. Khatri begins.

"Wait!" I say, raising my hand to stop him. "I want my girlfriend with me when I hear what you have to say. The nurse told me there were people in the waiting room for me and that I could see them as soon as you cleared me. You just said I'd be okay. So, they can come in now. Right?"

He purses his lips again. He's driving me crazy.

"What?" I ask, exasperated.

Dr. Khatri must feel sorry for me because he stands and moves towards the door, stopping just long enough to get a few pumps of hand sanitizer from a dispenser on the wall. He rubs the liquid around his palms with long, sweeping motions then carefully covers the back of his hands and his knuckles.

"Give me a minute," he says. "I'll be right back."

Finally. I'm relieved. I'm anxious to see Lottie. Her familiar touch will soothe me. I know it will. I was beginning to think Dr. Khatri wouldn't allow her to come in. He seemed hesitant. Thank goodness he heard me. I was ready to fight harder if I'd had to. I'm glad to be over that hump.

I lean my head back against the bed and look out the wide window while I wait. It's daytime, although I can't tell what time of day. The blinds are tilted to keep the brightness from overwhelming the room, but I see the silhouette of a trio of palm trees. They soothe me, too. The tropical setting here on the island feels like home. It's hard to believe that it once felt foreign. The palm trees, sandy beaches, and casual island locale seem like a family of sorts. One that keeps me safe and has my back. I don't hold it against Hideaway Isle that Nigel put me in the hospital. He's from Fox, anyway. I'll chalk that up to my troubled past rearing its ugly head. I suppose it was bound to happen at some point. It probably isn't possible to leave an entire life and childhood behind and expect that it won't follow you somehow. I suspect it always does in one way or another.

I don't have to wait long before I hear a soft knock on the door. *Lottie.* I'm going to be so ridiculously glad to see her pretty face. I'll smother it with kisses, just as soon as I apologize for letting Nigel's smarmy ass ruin our lunch date. I lean forward in bed in anticipation. I move too quickly at first, but the pain in my head slows me down. I push the pain away in favor of focusing on my best girl.

"Come in!" I say enthusiastically.

The large silver latch on the door sounds and begins to open. I watch eagerly for Lottie, but she isn't the first one to enter. It's Margot. Then Rags. They seem cautious. Sad, even.

"Hey, Basia," Margot says as she waits for Rags to clear the doorway and then closes the heavy door behind them. "How are you feeling, my friend?"

They both smile at me feebly. I'm confused, and I say as much.

"Where's Lottie?"

Margot looks at Rags for reassurance, then smiles back at me again. Rags keeps one hand on the small of Margot's back. He's steadying her, like Lottie often does for me. The physical touch is a reminder that he's there, both emotionally and physically. It's an anchor during tough times. It's a tangible part of the love they share, the same as those gestures are for Lottie and me.

"Can we sit with you, Basia?" Rags asks in his husky voice.

He gives me big brother vibes. I don't have a big brother, but if I did, he might be somewhere around Rags' age.

"Sure," I say quickly.

I aim to get the small talk out of the way and find out what's going on. There will be plenty of time for small talk when Lottie joins us. I'll be on edge until she arrives, anyway. I just want her here next to me. I want to feel her warm skin on mine. To smell her familiar scent. She's my home in this world.

"How's the head?" Rags asks as he pulls a chair close to the side of my bed. He motions for Margot to sit right on the bed with me.

"It's fine," I reply. "Well, it hurts. But I'll live. The doctor-- Dr. Khatri-- said I'll be okay. Why isn't Lottie here? Is she in the bathroom or something?"

Rags and Margot glance at each other again. For two

people who've been in the Navy, they aren't being very subtle right now. That worries me.

Margot gets comfortable in an open spot towards the bottom of my hospital bed, near my knees.

"Is this okay?" she asks.

"Yeah," I say.

It is okay. In fact, I appreciate Margot and Rags showing up for me. I'm surprised I have visitors. Surprised I have people around at all, for that matter. It feels like I've been a loner for a long time. That reminds me. I want to know about the slew of people Agnes referred to.

"Hey, who else is in the waiting room?" I ask. "My nurse, Agnes, who is really sweet, by the way, mentioned that there were several people out there waiting to see me."

Margot smiles, without looking at Rags this time. I'm not sure whether or not I should consider that progress. This slow roll out of information is frustrating. Margot and Rags are acting cagey the same way Agnes and Dr. Khatri did. That can't be good. Unless this is the way people with head injuries are typically treated.

I wish I had experience that could tell me what was normal and what wasn't for someone with an injury like mine. Maybe if I'd worked in a medical setting. Or if I'd taken a few medical classes in school. There was a health sciences career path at Fox Senior High. I didn't take it, though. I wasn't sure I'd find my way to college, so it didn't seem worth the time and effort. Looking back, I wish I'd focused on something in high school that would have given me better job opportunities. If there was a dip in the tourism industry on Hideaway Isle, I could lose my income from portrait painting and palm reading, and then I'm not sure what I'd fall back on. Waitressing, maybe. Kesha made it look easy. I could probably make do working at a restaurant. I doubt I'd earn as much though.

"She's right," Margot says, bringing me back to the present. She's wearing the same blue Navy t-shirt with white letters that she had on earlier. That must mean it's the same day. Good to know.

"Yeah?"

"There are quite a few of us here to see you," Margot continues. "We've been waiting on the okay to come in and visit."

"Who's here?" I ask.

Rags jumps in to finish Margot's thought. "Puck and Chely are out there. And Grandpa Herbert. Oh, and Chevelle, too." He chuckles nervously, which is odd for him. Rags isn't a nervous guy. "Cap wanted to come, but they insisted dogs weren't allowed in the hospital."

"He would have done it if they'd let him," Margot adds, also laughing nervously.

I shake my head.

"Look, guys, I appreciate all of you being here. I mean it. I do. But where's Lottie? Why aren't you mentioning her? And why won't you answer me when I ask about her? You're freaking me out."

Margot takes a deep breath, then places both of her hands over one of mine. She wraps her fingers delicately around the IV port that's attached to the top of my hand and covered in medical tape. She's gentle. It doesn't hurt. "We do owe you an explanation. That's what we've come to say."

"Well, we would have come to visit, anyway," Rags clarifies. "We want you to know we're here for you. For anything you may need."

"Right," Margot agrees. "But we do have some news to share. It isn't news of a good nature. It's…"

"Just spit it out already!" I exclaim.

7

UNDER PRESSURE

I'm staring at Margot's somber face, exasperated, when there's another knock on the door. *Lottie.* It has to be her this time. Where else would she go knowing that I'm here, injured? Our relationship is solid enough for me to count on her support. She wouldn't let me down in my time of need.

It's strange. Since waking up in the hospital a little while ago, my usually active intuition seems to be shut off. It isn't working like it's supposed to. I feel distanced from myself. Like the essence of me is back a stretch from my eyes. Is it the head injury? Or the effects of the medication they've given me? I wish I knew. It's almost like I'm sitting in an IMAX movie theater, but too close to the screen. As if I'm in the empty part of the theater down at the front. The part where they don't put seats because you can't see anything if you sit there. It's like I'm stuck there. In the dead zone. The action is giving me whiplash as I try to take it in from this wrong vantage point. I don't know how to get out. I don't know how to fix it.

"Lottie?" I say out loud.

Margot's face falls when I do. She looks genuinely pained. Rags doesn't look much better.

"I'm afraid not," Dr. Khatri says as he enters the room.

He stops, standing tall just inside the doorway. He pulls his lab coat together in the middle while balancing a clipboard under one arm. My eyes trace the blue script embroidered above his breast pocket that reads Dr. Yash Khatri. I wonder how anyone can forget his name. I'm pretty sure it's now burned into my memory. Trauma does that to a person. I know it does. Makes everything stand still and slow down. Although, maybe for some people, it has the opposite effect. Maybe it all becomes a blur and speeds up. Maybe those people can't remember more than Dr. K since their minds are on fast forward.

"Hello, doctor," Margot says. She's apparently taking the lead in whatever this is. "We've only been here a few minutes. We haven't had time to… talk."

Dr. Khatri raises his brows and opens his eyes so wide he reminds me of a Muppet. Gonzo, specifically. Or maybe Animal. I remember Pa saying how Jim Henson's Muppets were popular when he was a kid. He sometimes made me watch old episodes and movies when we weren't watching Superman. Suddenly, *The Muppets Take Manhattan* movie plays in my mind, clear as day. I can almost smell the RC Cola and the microwave popcorn. Act II was Pa's favorite brand. The human brain is such a strange organ.

I shake it off and tell myself to focus. But I don't form words fast enough.

"Understood," the doctor says. "Unfortunately, that talk will have to wait."

"What? Why?" I ask. "What are you talking about?"

Dr. Khatri steps closer to my bed. He forgot his hand sanitizer this time. Or is he supposed to do that on the way out? My mind isn't keeping up. I'm… confused.

"Scans are back," he says. "Basia, I might have spoken too soon about everything being okay, physically."

"But I'm fine," I say. "Except for a headache. That isn't going away."

"Sometimes it seems that way, like you are fine," he replies. "But remember how I said head injuries are tricky?"

"Yeah," I say.

"The brain can get jostled inside the head. When it does, bleeding can happen, leading to increased pressure over time. Sometimes, the bleeding and increased pressure are delayed. It can take time to cause obvious problems."

"Is that what's happening in Basia's case?" Margot asks.

"I'm right here," I say. "I'm not just a case. I'm a person."

Margot squeezes my hand gently. "I'm sorry. You certainly are. Let me rephrase that. Doctor, is that what's happening to Basia?"

He nods. "We see evidence of a subdural hematoma. A blood clot that's growing."

Rags slumps his shoulders and suddenly looks much

smaller in his chair. It looks like the air has been deflated out of him. "Aw, man," he mutters. "Tough break."

Margot looks ultra-serious, like she's been tasked with managing me and intends to give it her all. I appreciate that. She inspires confidence. She's smart and capable, and I believe she has my best interests at heart. If Mama can't be here, I'm left with several capable substitutes, I suppose. If only Lottie...

"What do we do now?" Margot asks.

"We need to prep her for surgery," Dr. Khatri replies.

My heart sinks, becoming hard and dense like a stone. Fear courses through me. Now I know what deer in headlights feel like. The shock of my imminent demise is startling, to say the least. I'm too young for this. Too *good* for this. Aren't I? What did I do to deserve it? I know I left home. I know I should have kept in touch with my family. Yet I don't know anything, really. I just wish I could worm my way out of this predicament. Anything but this. It doesn't feel fair.

"On my head?" I ask. "You want to operate on my head?"

He nods again, looking directly at me this time. Dr. Khatri steps closer to my bed and places one hand on my shoulder. I can tell he cares, but I'm the one he wants to cut into. The urgency isn't the same for him. "Basia, I know an operation sounds scary. If there were any other way, we'd do it. If we could simply watch and wait, we would. In fact, that's exactly what we've been doing for the past few hours. But now, this is an emergency. Your brain is in trauma. Blood is pooling and your brain cells are swimming in it. We have to get in there and relieve the pressure, or..."

"Or what?" I ask, my face balling up. I want to cry, but my tear ducts are bone dry like the sand dunes near the shore on our little island. So close to the water, yet it's inaccessible.

"Or you won't survive," he says matter-of-factly.

Dr. Khatri's words hit me like a punch to the gut. And with them, the realization that Nigel did this to me. That he did it out of hate. Because I'm gay. How utterly despicable. The weight of it crashes over and around me. I want Lottie so badly at this moment.

Margot throws herself over me, hugging me tightly. I feel numb, emotionally, anyway. My body feels odd, but I can't quite describe it. Maybe the thing that's wrong with my head is affecting my body. Maybe it's affecting my thinking. And my intuition. I hug Margot back, and I quickly come to terms with the surgery. I don't want them cutting into me. But I'll do what I have to do. It sounds like it truly is do or die. What choice do I have? I trust Dr. Khatri, so I guess I have to make the leap and hope I make it safely to the other side. I mean the other side of the surgery, but as I think the words, I can't help but think about the *other* other side-- the hereafter. Even so, what I'm worried about is Lottie. Something is wrong. I don't need intuition to feel that. Margot and Rags are making it pretty obvious.

"Okay," I say to Dr. Khatri. "I understand."

He breathes a sigh of relief. He must have expected me to fight him about this. Or to yell and scream. I don't know what he expected, but I'm too shocked to do any of that. Besides, I know he's trying to help me. What good would it do to waste time struggling with him when he could be saving me instead?

"I'm glad," the doctor says and gives my shoulder a squeeze.

"Will you perform the procedure?" Margot asks through tears. Rags stands and walks to the other side of my bed so he can put a strong hand on her arm. He looks teary eyed, too.

I'm surprised to see them tearing up like this. We've only known each other for a few short weeks. Margot is Lottie's big sister, but even they hadn't been close for years. I suppose the events of late have served to bond us all closer together. We don't have many older relatives in the picture, which makes it all the more important that us younger folks show up for each other. And of course, my family is in Wisconsin, estranged. I wonder if Margot already thinks of me as family. I hope she does. And I guess Rags looks at me as family by extension. That's sweet.

We all look at Dr. Khatri expectantly as we wait for him to answer Margot's question.

"I will," he confirms. "Along with another neurosurgeon, Dr. Ian Marcellus. He will assist me. He's getting prepped right now."

I hesitate, waiting for more. Dr. Khatri takes the cue.

"Basia," he says with a new shoulder squeeze. "This is what we do nearly every day. We've been doing it for years. Dr. Marcellus and I have been trained at some of the top schools in the country-- him at Vanderbilt University in Nashville, Tennessee, and me at Mayo Clinic in Minneapolis. You're in good hands. I promise."

It feels like my head is swimming. I'm not sure if it's because Dr. Khatri used that word, but it seems that things are sloshing around in there. "Okay," I say.

I stare at a spot on the floor, tracing the small square pattern in my mind. It feels like I'm losing my grip on waking consciousness. Like I can't quite say what I want to. I'm still thinking about things and processing words, but there seems to be a disconnect between my thinking and my speech. Margot sees my struggle and takes over. She stands and steps close to the doctor.

"She doesn't have next of kin," Margot says. "Can she appoint a decision maker?"

The doctor hesitates. "There could be questions of capacity," he says. "If not now, then very soon."

Margot steps close to me and gets in my face. "Basia?" she says. "Basia, honey, I need you to choose someone to make medical decisions for you in the event that you aren't able to do so for yourself? Do you understand?"

I nod.

"Lottie," I say. "Lottie Callaway… my…"

Margot puts one finger over her mouth. She's in soldier mode now, handling things. I must be looking bad because Dr. Khatri steps out to gather more personnel. When he does, Margot comes all the way to my ear, whispering her words in deep.

"Basia, Lottie isn't available. Something has happened. I'll tell you about it later. I need you to trust me, okay. I'm going to take care of you."

I shake my head. No, no. Definitely not.

"Not later. Now," I manage.

"There isn't time," she says, grabbing my other hand and squeezing it.

So much squeezing. I feel like a newborn baby that everyone is poking and squeezing to be sure I'm showing the proper amount of vigor, whatever that means. What the hell? I appreciate the attention, but this is getting me riled up.

"Basia," Rags tries. They're both glancing from me to the door. The sense of urgency comes across loud and clear. "A group of people is about to barge in that door and take you down the hall to the operating room. If you want one of us to make medical decisions for you, you've got to tell the doctor as soon as he gets back."

"Do you understand?" Margot asks. "They need someone. Do you want me to give them contact information for your family in Wisconsin? Can you tell me how to reach them?"

I take this in. Maybe I should tell Margot how to contact Mama. I know my old home phone number by heart. Mama may have gone through men like she did dirty underwear, but she stayed in one place for most of my childhood. I suspect she still lives in the same old, run down cottage on a hill by the river. The tan land-line phone probably still hangs on a wall behind the kitchen table, its tightly coiled cord dangling below. I think my mind is working well enough to recite the phone number, although I can't be sure. The gap between my thought process and my speech seems to be widening by the minute.

I nod my understanding, staring up at Margot's wide eyes and wavy hair. I'm struck by the similarities between that old phone cord and Margot's hair. Does that mean my mental faculties are deteriorating? Margot has a section of her locks fastened with a barrette and pulled back from her face, but the waves still cascade around her shoulders. I remember her saying how much tighter her curls are here in the Florida humidity than they are in other parts of the world. I also remember Rags saying how much he loves Margot's natural curls. I'm touched and inspired by the love Margot and Rags have for each other. I believe Lottie and I share the same kind of love.

My thoughts wander back to my love. They're never far.

I can't help but wonder what Margot means when she says Lottie isn't available. I deserve a better explanation than that. The comment doesn't hold up in this dicey situation. It's feeble. Weak. I might be feeling feeble and weak myself, but my thoughts circle back around to the fact that I deserve better. What if my life really is in grave danger? What if, by some horrible stroke of fate, I die in this hospital today, right on the operating table? I deserve to know where Lottie is.

"Lottie," I say weakly.

I sound forlorn and helpless. I can hear it in my voice. I hate it.

"Basia, please," Rags implores. "It's better if you don't know the details right now. You need your strength up for surgery. It will take a lot out of you."

"He's exactly right," Margot adds. "We need to focus on healthcare decisions, Basia. Who do you want to make decisions for you if you aren't able? Please, Lottie would want us to help you. *Let us* help you."

A wave of nausea washes over me. It's all encompassing. All of a sudden, it feels like I'll drown in it. I double over, barely able to keep my eyes open because I need to close them to cope with the nausea and worsening headache. If I didn't believe it before, I do now. Something is badly wrong with me. My entire body feels uncomfortable. It's as if I'm being swallowed by something. In a flash, I imagine the scene that took place when the boat from Lottie's tour company capsized and those people were pinned underwater. This must be how they felt, only with fluid-filled lungs and no chance for a desperately needed breath of air. My mind shows me an assortment of disturbing images, including the fiery scene with billowing smoke I saw Nigel and his friend running from. Every single image is ominous and morbid. In every scene, people die. I'm afraid.

The metal latch sounds loudly and Dr. K steps inside. Oh, no. I no longer remember his full name. And here I told him I'd call him by it. I hope he won't be offended that I can't remember. Maybe I won't have to tell him. Maybe I can get by without saying his name.

"We're ready," he announces.

"She hasn't named a decision maker yet," Margot reports. "But I'd like to ask her one more time while you're here to record her answer."

"Go ahead," the doc says.

He gestures to someone outside the door, telling them to wait. I get the idea there are nurses and doctors out there. Although, he might be motioning to some of my other visitors. Maybe they'll be allowed to come in. Maybe it's Lottie.

"Lottie? Are you out there?" I ask. Only I'm not sure the words come out like they should.

Margot gets all in my face again, talking slow and loud as if I'm a baby.

"Basia, honey, I told you. Lottie isn't here," she says. "This is important. Please listen closely, okay?"

I nod obediently.

"Basia, you're going into surgery to repair a blood clot in your brain. It's serious. We need to know who you want to make medical decisions for you if you aren't able to make them for yourself. Okay? Who do you want to do that?"

"Lottie," I reply.

Margot leans her head back in frustration, then looks down at me again. "Anyone else?" she asks. "Besides Lottie."

I scowl, although I don't know why. My head is pounding and I'm terribly sick. I think I might vomit. I don't get why this is so important. Margot is hammering me on the question of who will be my medical decision maker. And I don't understand why. Part of me wants Mama to come here and take care of me like she did when I broke my arm as a kid. But the other part doesn't want her to find out I'm gay or to be hurtful to Lottie and her family. I don't think I'm in any frame of mind to make that call right now, anyway. Finally, I decide to name Margot my decision maker. Maybe then she'll tell me about Lottie.

"Margot," I say, pointing up to her and poking her neck with my finger. "Besides Lottie, I want Margot."

I slump into a fetal position on the bed, nearly all my energy expended to say those few words. I hope they're happy.

"Did you hear that?" Margot asks the doctor.

"I did," he says. "I'm notating it in her record as we speak."

"I'll be here," Margot says, "for whatever she needs. I'm not going anywhere."

I hear her saying nice things about me and how she'll

stick with me. I'm glad. My eyes open and fix on Margot's back. I stare at her long curly hair and her strong shoulders framed by her blue t-shirt. I think about what a good mama she'll be someday. She and Rags will have beautiful children, and my Lottie will be an aunt. I want to be around to see those beautiful babies. To be an aunt, too.

Unable to help myself, I drift off. To where, I don't know, but I go far, far away.

Lights out.

Heaven, help me.

PART II

CRUSH

8

BUMP IN THE NIGHT

When I was a kid, back in Fox, Wisconsin, I used to dream every night. Some dreams were good, like the ones about playing kickball with Pa or others about running along the riverbank near our house in the summer and catching crawdads from under rocks. The good dreams were made of the stuff all kids love. They were simple pleasures, full to the brim with wishes I'd ask for again and again. And sometimes, my good dreams came true.

The bad dreams, though, showed up often. They kept me trapped, held prisoner by my own mind and terrified to fall asleep. I'd lay awake, petrified of the moment when I could no longer keep my eyes open and sleep would take me. It was a sad, cruel fact of life in those days.

There was one particular wolf who showed up in my dreams again and again. His name was Echo, and his dastardly face will never leave my recollection. Echo's coat was light silver with darker gray around his muzzle and paws. He was pretty to look at, but he was mean as a snake. His presence terrified me. I remember the way he'd enter my room, head hung low and tentative, but his timid demeanor was for show. There was nothing tentative about him. He'd slide around the corner and through the doorway to my room, pushing the door open with his powerful head if it had been closed when he'd arrived. I remember the chill that ran up and down my spine when our eyes met, Echo staring into the depths of my vulnerable soul.

Usually, I woke up screaming before the wolf had a chance to do anything to me. The simple threat of what his primal capabilities could do was enough to send me fleeing. I soon learned how to wake myself up by moving a body part, often by lifting my head ever so slightly off the pillow. It took a lot of trial and error and didn't always work, but eventually, I could get away from my bad dreams by my own volition. It was a huge relief to have a way out. Knowing there was an escape from Echo's clutches made it easier to fall asleep most nights. Except I was never truly free because he'd return again and again.

Mama would tend to me when I woke up in tears. I guess that's much like being sick or injured, as far as she was concerned. My distress was enough to get her attention for a little while. I've sometimes wondered if I created Echo in my subconscious mind just so Mama would come and sit with me each time I had a bad dream. I still don't know for sure. The dreams about Echo started when Pa still lived at home with us, but they persisted through two stepdads and a host of changes in our lives. That dreadful wolf kept returning to haunt me, slinking into my room and approaching the foot of my bed as I lay terrified. Sometimes, I'd see him dart around the edges of the bed, crouching in preparation to attack when I least expected it, his sharp white fangs glimmering between his soft lips. I can still remember his features in such sharp detail.

As my ability to control aspects of my dream world grew, I'd tell Echo no or to stop and get back. That held him off now and then, but it wasn't until Aunt Portia gave me a bit of advice that the wolf finally turned tail and went away for good. She told me that I was in charge of my dreams. Completely, totally in charge. At the time, that was news to me. She also told me that if I needed help in a dream, I could call her and she'd come to my aid. I took her up on that offer, and sure enough, Aunt Portia would assist whenever Echo reared his lousy head. That woman taught me a lot about fine tuning my intuition and psychic abilities. I'm grateful to her, no doubt. When she told me that It was time to get rid of Echo for good, I readied myself to follow her instructions.

On the final night, after sneaking into my room while I was asleep, the wolf had the nerve to lunge toward one of the stuffed animals on my bed. It was a plush bunny rabbit that Pa had given me when I was a baby, pink and white with plastic eyes. That bunny rabbit was my very favorite toy and my most prized possession. It was tangible proof that Pa had loved me once. I wasn't about to let Echo take it away from me. When the savage beast went for the toy, something inside me snapped. It was my breaking point. It may sound childish, but at the time, the decision meant everything to me. After years of nighttime misery at the wolf's hands, I was ready to face him head on, once and for all.

I remember it like it was yesterday. Instead of avoiding eye contact with Echo, I sought it. Instead of moving to flee, I stood strong and firm, unyielding. I didn't even need to call for Aunt Portia. Every ounce of my being was done with him. I told the wolf in no uncertain terms that he had better not come back ever again. I told him I wasn't scared of him anymore, and that he had no power over me. I could feel the certainty of my words all the way down to the tips of my toes. Echo must have felt it, too, because for the first time, he cowered. Knowing he had been beaten at his own game, he scooted out of my bedroom and out of my life. It felt glorious to rid myself of the nuisance. I felt powerful and strong. Unafraid. It was a turning point in my life. And it was an important lesson to learn as I moved into my teenage years. I'd need that resolve to face the hardships to come.

As I float through an unusual dream-like state in the here and now, I'm unsure whether to be afraid. I remember being with Margot and Rags, and I remember Dr. Khatri saying there was a blood clot in my head that he had to operate on right away if I wanted to survive. I'm glad that I can remember his full name now: Dr. Yash Khatri. I feel like myself again. My thoughts are whole. But I get the strange feeling that my thoughts aren't coming from my brain. They're disconnected, yet still intact. I wonder if I'm in surgery right now. Dare I say it, but I wonder if I'm having some type of out-of-body experience. I've heard of people who say they left their body while it was injured or operated on. Have I joined their ranks?

I tell myself to remain calm and survey my

surroundings. That's got to be the first step. If Aunt Portia really was right and I can control my dreams, I might be able to control this space, too. It's worth a shot, anyway. My history in standing up to Echo gives me confidence. Slowly, I look around. It's dark. There are a million tiny lights in the distance. They look like stars. I think I'm in space. I feel weightless and unencumbered. My body sort of floats, like it does in water. Only I'm not sure this is my body at all. It might just be the essence of me, for lack of a better description. I might be in another form than what I'm used to. Funny enough, I still feel like myself. I am me, even here. Even now.

From a distance, I hear what sounds like angels singing. I don't understand what they're singing about. The words are foreign. Latin, maybe? Their pure, enchanting melody draws me in. I immediately move towards the sound. As I glide through space, I'm reminded of the stories in Greek mythology about sirens calling to sailors and how the sounds of their voices proved irresistible. I kind of get it all of a sudden. These angelic voices make me want to go to them. To hear more. To see their faces. I want to know the beings who are making this beautiful music. I want it to wrap me up and surround every inch of me. I'm not afraid of the singers or this unusual place in the Universe. I feel at home here, as if I've been here before. Truth be told, I feel more at ease here than I do in my body on Earth. This place feels somehow more evolved. Gone are the problems and burdens that typically weigh on me. Everything feels perfectly okay here. I might like to stick around.

As I near the sound of the ethereal singing, a large

building with ornate stained glass windows appears. It might be a church, although I don't get the feeling that anyone would be excluded from this place like they were from Mama's church back home in Fox. There, I wouldn't have been welcome if they'd known I was gay. In this building, though, I get the distinct sense none of that matters. I'm more than welcome here. The large, wooden double doors are open, so I step inside. Immediately, an elaborate scene unfolds in front of me. I'm not sure if it's a figment of my imagination or not, but it's comforting, nonetheless. Rows of pews frame a grand sanctuary like none I've ever seen before. The whole experience feels like it's speaking to me, personally. Healing a part of me that I didn't know needed healing. I'm overwhelmed with gratitude. I want more. I need more.

Right away, I notice that the singing is coming from a beautiful lady whose presence occupies the entire front of the room. Her hair is long and red, and she wears a flowing white gown. Around her shoulders is the most intricate, lovely shawl. It's a deep crimson red with a delicate golden edge. It almost looks like wings that have been tucked neatly behind her. I wouldn't be surprised if wings opened up majestically and the creature took flight. Nothing that I'm seeing is what I would have expected, but it soothes my heart and soul.

An organ is positioned near the angelic figure, and it plays itself in the background. The organ music is perfectly timed with the singer's voice, even though no one touches its keys. One might think this whole scene would be creepy. It's anything but. This pretty, singing lady is so dignified, so otherworldly, that I feel incredibly humbled and honored to be in her presence. She bobs and turns with the beat, swaying gently as her whole essence brings forth the heavenly music. I approach cautiously, drawn like a moth to a flame. I'm mesmerized. Slowly, slowly I move forward. When I reach the front of the sanctuary, the woman turns to look at me. Her eyes meet mine and she smiles, although she doesn't stop singing. I open my mouth to greet her, then realize speech isn't needed here. This won't be the kind of communication I'm used to.

"Hello," she says telepathically.

I get the message, even though her words are sent to my mind silently. I'm awestruck by the efficiency and raw power of what's happening. I should have known that speech was cumbersome and wouldn't be needed in a setting like this. My psychic abilities and intuition aren't about speech. I've practiced for this, without even realizing it.

"Hello," I return with my mind, nodding as if to volley the message across the short expanse between us.

The lady smiles even more broadly, her face aglow with affection and kindness toward me. I don't think I know her, exactly. Yet she's familiar to me. I wonder if she really is an angel. She's certainly wise. I suspect I could ask her anything and she'd know the answer. I wonder why I've been brought here to her. Or sent here. Or whatever. I'm finding more and more that words can't adequately convey what I'm experiencing.

"Welcome home," she communicates. "You're safe here. We've been waiting for you."

For a split second, I wonder who she's referring to when she uses the word we, plural. But I feel so loved and at peace that I don't really care. All my worries are falling away. It almost seems like I can't remember my Earthly concerns anymore.

I nod again to acknowledge her welcome. "Who are you?" I ask.

"No name, because names aren't needed here, but you can think of me as Charmiene," she replies without words.

I like knowing what to call her. Maybe I'm still clinging to the conventions I'm used to, but I don't blame myself. I'm going to keep calling this lady Charmiene for the foreseeable future. Maybe one day, I'll be ready to let names go. If I stay here, that is. I don't know yet. I'm not ready to make those kinds of decisions.

Charmiene is slowly shifting and moving in front of me, as if her energy must swirl constantly to fuel itself. It reminds me of an avatar on a video game. I let out a little laugh at the thought. She doesn't mind. She just waits and keeps smiling.

"Am I dead?" I blurt, surprising myself.

Even more alarming is the way I don't really care if I am or not. If this is the afterlife, it isn't so bad. It feels like home, a safe and tranquil place.

She doesn't answer me, but she turns to one side as a giant picture window opens up. Charmiene motions for me to stand beside her and to look through the window. I do, and a recognizable scene appears. It's the hospital on Hideaway Isle. I see an operating room where a group of people are working feverishly on someone. They're all wearing gloves, masks, surgical caps, and scrubs. They're focused intently on the patient, clearly giving it their all.

I'm immediately impressed by their diligent efforts. No one is doing anything halfway.

Suddenly, I think about my own surgery and I wonder why they didn't airlift me to Miami. The hospital in Hideaway Isle has a good reputation, but not like the medical centers on the mainland. Our little island hospital might not be equipped to handle blood clots and brain bleeds. Isn't that kind of neurosurgery higher level? Charmiene nods slowly, urging me to look closer at the scene through the picture window.

"What?" I ask silently. "Why are you showing me this?"

She gently guides my attention back to the scene. Then I see it. My blonde, sun-soaked hair peeks beneath the black ring they have attached to my skull. My eyes are closed, and tubes run through my throat, but I recognize myself. My tan skin looks like lightly browned butter, smooth and youthful. That's my body down there. That's… me. The shock of seeing myself from a distance like this gives me a jolt. A jolt of what, I don't know. But it's jarring. I instinctively move towards the picture window. I want to protect my body that's strapped to the operating table. I want to see that it's taken good care of.

My attention moves to the doctors and nurses performing the procedure. As I study the group of them, I recognize Dr. Khatri. He's suited up with his head down, his hands working tirelessly on the top of my head. Another doctor, younger and shorter, works diligently at his side. Dr. Marcellus. I see. He's good, too. They both know what they're doing, as do the nurses, anesthesiologists, and everyone else present. They're real-life superheroes, giving it their all to fix me. To fix my body.

"Why am I here?" I ask Charmiene, without looking away from the surgical scene.

She moves closer, and I feel a presence against my back. She gently turns me, and another picture window opens. The angelic singing and organ playing continues in the background. As my awareness expands, I don't lose any layers as more are added. It's fascinating, really. I wish I could come to this place whenever I wish. In meditation maybe, or at night when I dream.

I know that Charmiene's answer to my question will become known when I look at the next window. I'm not sure I'm ready, but she seems to think I am. Gently, she says, "Basia, you have a choice to make."

9

LIGHT AND WEIGHT

The gravity of her comment isn't lost on me. Even in this ethereal, airy state, I feel the seriousness of what I'm facing. I do have a choice to make. A big one. Do I stay? Or do I go? My life as I knew it could be over. Maybe it is over and the doctors' attempts are futile. I don't think so, though. I think I can still go back to my body if I want to. I do want to. Although, it would be awfully nice to stay.

Focusing my attention on the second picture window that has appeared, a new scene comes into view. Charmiene doesn't explain or summarize it. She doesn't do anything to prepare me for what I'm about to see. She just lets me watch as she continues to twist and move to the celestial music. I hesitate for a moment, unsure of what to expect. The surgical scene remains in the first window. It's jarring to look at, even now that I've taken it in. I assume the second scene will be equally disconcerting. I steel myself, then when I've gathered the necessary courage, I look fully, ready to absorb whatever awaits.

"Look," Charmiene communicates, reinforcing my resolve.

And I do. I see a beautiful, peaceful garden. It's beside a lovingly restored white farmhouse perched atop a high hill and overlooking a clean, wide river. A silver suspension bridge stands tall in the distance. Beyond that, a cityscape peeks from the valley. It isn't Florida, that's for sure. This is somewhere else. Somewhere with a cooler climate and four seasons. The trees and flowers aren't like the ones on Hideaway Isle. I allow myself to be immersed in this scene, moving all the way into it. It's relaxing and safe. I don't have the reluctance that I did about getting too close to the scene from the hospital. This one is different. I step in, feeling soft grass beneath my feet. I glance back at Charmiene, who waves a hand to reassure me. I face forward, letting myself see and feel it all.

There's a long, rectangular swimming pool in the middle of this garden. The water within sparkles against the sun's rays and invites me to take a dip. Chaise lounges are grouped in clusters of two or three, all flanking the sides of the pool. Potted plants surround the chairs and create a cozy ambiance. I'm not sure I'm ready to immerse myself in the swimming pool yet, but I sit down and get comfortable on one of the lounge chairs. I ease down onto it, my being completely relaxed. This garden feels somehow restorative, as if I'll recharge by just hanging out here for a while. I'm enjoying the warm sun and gentle breeze when I sense the presence of a visitor. Someone else is here with me.

I prop myself up on one elbow to see who it is. The

sun is bright and at first, it blocks my view. I raise a hand over my eyes to shade my view and dim the brightness. As I do so, I'm well aware that all of the physical movements and sensations I'm experiencing may be generated from my own mind. This is probably easier to cope with when it seems simple and recognizable. I go with it. A figure comes into view and walks toward me. It's a man. I can tell from his gait and large stature. I don't think I know him. At least, not right off. He comes slowly closer, taking tentative steps.

"Basia?" he asks without words.

When his message reaches me, I'm overcome with emotion. I know immediately who it is. I can hardly believe it. It's my own Pa, Greg Guthrie. My daddy. I haven't seen him since I was a tiny girl. And he's here. In this mystical garden that Charmiene has led me to. I'm not sure what to say or do. I'm frozen, overwhelmed.

Tears spring to my eyes, although I know I'm not in a physical body and don't even have eyes here. The feeling is similar, though. A rush comes from somewhere inside me and pours toward my face, desperate to get out. The emotion wants an outlet. It's brought forth whether I like it or not. There's no holding it back. I'm not sure there would be even if I was in my body. I'm so shocked to see Pa here. If he's here, that must mean…

"Pa?" I reply.

He steps closer, coming into full view. He looks just like I remember him. He's fit and muscular, his wavy black hair curling over his ears. His big brown eyes beam with joy at seeing me. He even has a pipe in one hand. I close my eyes for a second and I swear I can smell his old familiar cherry tobacco.

"It's me," he offers. "Is it really you?"

I stand, gathering myself up to present myself to my daddy. I feel like I should be better dressed or something. Absurd, I know. It's just that this meeting feels monumental. It's a really big deal. I hadn't heard from or seen Pa for so long. If he's-- it's hard to say it-- *dead*, that might explain why. What if he wasn't a bad guy, but instead unable to come see me? That would change things. A lot. I'd have to rewrite my entire history. Mama might have to rewrite hers, too.

"It is me," I return. "Your daughter. Your little girl."

Pa opens his arms and I rush to him without any pause. He wraps me in a tight embrace. As I feel his strong hands against my arms and my head against his chest, I remember what this felt like, before. I had forgotten, but I remember it now, right down to the way Pa's chin feels resting against my head. It feels glorious. Like a much-needed reset button. I've apparently needed my daddy. We hug long and hard, him kissing the top of my head, just like he used to. When I'm finally ready to pull back, I take a good look at him. The lines in his face are the same. The fine details that were somewhere in my buried memories have resurfaced. It's like he never left.

"Basia, baby girl, I've missed you so much," he says. "I never wanted to leave you."

I believe him. How could I not?

"What happened?" I ask. "Where did you go?"

His energy shifts, moving lower and sadder. He hangs his head.

"I made some bad choices," he begins. "I know that now. From here, I can see things clearly. I'm sorry for the hurt my actions caused you."

I'm confused.

"What actions, Pa? I don't understand."

"Your mom and I couldn't make things work. We didn't get along. We fought over petty grievances. We were too immature to appreciate what we had. I wish things had been better."

As he explains, images flood my mind. It's as if Pa is sharing them with me, to give me a more complete picture. I see him and Mama, riding in an old beaten-up car together. It must be a time before I was born, because Mama's hair was longer than I've ever seen it. She always said she'd cut it short when I was born. The two of them look happy as they ride along, but then things change. Next, I see them eating together at the kitchen table when I was a baby in Mama's arms. They're angry with each other, their hurts and misunderstandings hanging around them like thick fog. I wince. It's distressing to see, especially because I also remember feeling it from them live and in person. The images speed up, one after another moving into my consciousness. In a short period, these images have painted a complete picture. Mama and Pa loved each other deeply, but they didn't have the right role models and life experiences to succeed in their marriage. It wasn't anyone's fault. They simply weren't evolved enough to do the right things. They'd done their best. They'd split up for the good of everyone involved.

"I see," I communicate. "I don't blame you."

It surprises me as I admit it. Up until now, I probably would have blamed Pa for leaving us. Scratch that. I *definitely* would have blamed him. But he seems so genuine and sincere now. He isn't the same. At least, he isn't the man Mama made out to be such a villain. From this perspective, he isn't a villain at all. Mama never explained things the way Pa just did. I suppose Mama didn't have the capacity to do it this way, so I can't be mad at her either. It is what it is. I just wish I'd known sooner.

"How did you get here?" I ask. "Are you… dead?"

At this, Pa seems to want to defer to Charmiene. Until now, I wasn't sure he was aware of her presence. I turn and look. She's still back there, and the music plays on in the background. She nods slowly, giving Pa permission to share.

"Yes, Basia," he says telepathically. "I left my Earthly body less than a year after your mom and I broke up. It was my own fault. I had been drinking one night while working a temporary job in Grand Rapids. I got into a car, and I crashed it into a tree. I died at the scene."

He shows me the events in a series of images. The cruel reality cuts me like a knife. I thought I'd be glad to know why Pa hadn't come back, but knowing that he died makes me incredibly sad. I'm sad for my child self who grew up thinking her Pa didn't care about her. I'm sad for Mama, who is apparently destined to wade through a string of bad husbands when she was probably grieving the loss of her first true love. And I'm sad for Pa because his life was cut short. He missed out on so much.

"Did Mama know?" I inquire. It's an important question.

"No, she didn't. She *doesn't.* I didn't have an ID on me when I was killed. My body was cremated by the State. My ashes were spread over Lake Michigan along with those of a handful of other unidentified bodies."

I take a step back from Pa as I try to process this heavy news. It truly does change everything. I need time to sort through the implications. All the times I had imagined him off somewhere with a new family, having forgotten about us… well, I was wrong. It will take some effort to repair the damage that was done.

"Were you looking down on us?" I ask.

At this, Pa smiles his familiar smile, and I can't help but smile myself. With pleasure, he sends me another series of images, this time they're scenes from after he died. My fifth grade recorder concert, my middle school basketball tryouts, birthdays, holidays, and more. He saw it all. An overwhelming sensation of what I can only describe as pure love washes over me and wraps me up. In a whirlwind of emotion and sharing, things are made right between me and Pa. I forgive him. And for the first time in a long time, I know in the depths of my soul that he loves and cherishes me. It's the healing I've needed for far too long. Mixed with the love, I feel pride. Gratitude. Wholeness. I feel seen and heard. I feel incredible.

"I think of you often," I say. "I remember the things you used to love-- Jimmy Buffet, Superman, and the Packers."

He seems pleased by this, but also like he already knew.

"Jimmy Buffet is one of my favorite singers, too," I add. "Living in the Keys, his music is everywhere. You'd enjoy it, if you could somehow be there. And the Packers, well, I know they'll always be your favorite, but maybe you'd like the Miami Dolphins, too."

To this, he doesn't hesitate. "Basia, I already am there. I'm always with you."

Pa and I stand together for a long time in the garden, gazing out at the pool, the river, and the bridge and the city in the distance. It's pleasant. But we both know that we can't stay here forever. Not like this, exactly. Like Charmiene said, I have a decision to make. I think I get it now. I can stay here, with Pa, or I can return to my body. And it's up to me.

As if on cue, a trio of figures approaches to join us. They come into view more quickly than Pa did. I recognize them immediately. It's Grandpa Guthrie, Pa's dad. Next to him is-- *oh, aw*-- it's my sweet Aunt Portia. I didn't know she had passed. What a shame. The third figure is one I never met in person when he was alive, but I feel like I know him. It's Lottie's Grandpa Vern.

Lottie.

Her name sends me into an entirely new realm. I've been so affected by what I've seen and experienced that I haven't even thought about my dear, sweet Lottie. A pang of guilt hits me, but the loved ones around me send what feels like a giant group hug to melt the guilt away. They're right. I shouldn't feel guilty. But it's time I focus squarely on her. I need to know where she is. I need to get back to her. I could never leave Lottie. Not even to be with Pa. Surely, he understands that. He wants what's best for me. And one hundred percent, what's best for me is Lottie Callaway.

I'm going back to my body. I want to live.

Meeting my heightened level of awareness, the music in the background changes. Charmiene stops singing. Instead, a chorus of violins takes front and center as cellos rise and fall beneath them. The melody builds, buoying me.

"Hello, all," I volley to the others, nodding my head their way. "I'm happy to see you, but I can't stay here. I have to go back. For Lottie. I want to be with her. I want to spend the rest of my life with her. I'll return someday, when Lottie and I have raised a family and grown old and gray together."

They all smile so big and broadly, I suspect their positive energy could light up the night sky. They're with me. They support me. Pa smiles biggest of all, and he truly looks like a proud papa.

"Go to her," Pa says. "Live your life. We're never far away, Basia. Remember that. Godspeed, my child. You are so loved."

I wave, hurrying so I don't lose my nerve.

It strikes me as odd that Lottie's mom, Annie, didn't come to greet me along with the others, but I don't dwell on it. I remember Puck saying he thought he sometimes heard her voice in his ear. And Lottie and Margot both claim to have seen her in their dreams. Since she made the effort to communicate with them, it seems she would have come to see me. Who am I to guess how such things work, though?

I step out of the garden scene and rejoin Charmiene. The music grows louder. It feels like the heavens are rejoicing that I've chosen to fight for my life on Earth. That I've chosen to fight for my love and the beautiful life we'll live together. I turn to Charmiene and reaffirm my decision.

"I want to go back," I say. "To my life. To my love."

10

WAVES

I stand ready. My choice has been made. My chest swells with pride at knowing it was my choice to make, and that I did the right thing. Lottie will be so happy that I decided to stay. I can't wait to tell her all about this. Is it a near-death experience that I've just had? Perhaps it will strengthen my intuition. Or change the course of my life in some meaningful way.

Knowing what happened to Pa will certainly allow me to see things differently from here on out. I'm going to call Mama and tell her what happened to me, and to him. No, I'm going to *visit* Mama and tell her in person what happened. She deserves to hear it firsthand. Even if she doesn't believe me, I have to try to tell her. Maybe we can contact the authorities in Grand Rapids and somehow confirm what I've learned. That might give Mama a new lease on life. Maybe she could even get into talk therapy and work through her issues. It could be a fresh start. But first, I have to get out of here and back to my body in that operating room. I need to show vigor and responsiveness, so Drs. Khatri and Marcellus know to keep fighting on my behalf. I don't want to screw around and wait too long. I'd hate to choose to stay, then end up unable to. That would be one of the greatest tragedies imaginable. I won't let that be my story.

After hearing my decision, Charmiene nods slowly, then turns and gestures to yet another picture window.

What now? I'm growing impatient. I want to get moving, before it's too late. She picks up on my irritation but doesn't react. Charmiene is probably far too evolved to let anything upset her. Lovingly, yet firmly, she insists that I look. I sigh, not with my body, but with my energy. Then I follow her gaze and look. Instantly, my heart sinks. The scene in this window isn't a beautiful sanctuary or a peaceful garden. It's nothing of the sort. I recognize it, though.

There, black smoke billows from tall buildings. The blackness gathers itself up like a tidal wave and barrels forward, swallowing everything in its path. It's the exact same scene I saw while Lottie and I were eating lunch downtown. The one that forced itself into my consciousness when Nigel and his friend entered the restaurant patio. The one that seemed like a premonition of events to come.

"What is this?" I ask. "I've seen this before, while I was awake. But why?"

Charmiene is apparently a fan of showing rather than telling. I notice that she doesn't answer my questions directly. Instead, she shows me images, scenes, and familiar people that answer my queries. I suppose I'm not in a position to complain. My time with Charmiene has been very enlightening. I'm grateful to her for the guidance. Besides, she might be my personal guardian angel. I'm sure she knows best. I want to keep the lines of communication between us open. I want her to remain firmly on my side. She turns me back to the third picture window so that I can watch what happens.

As the events unfold in front of me, I again get the overwhelming feeling of tears rushing to my eyes, even though I don't have eyes here. The emotion wells up in the area of my eyes and head, ready to burst out. I look more closely, and I see people running for their lives as the wall of smoke and debris chases them down. Some trip and fall. Others encounter obstacles that slow them down. Even the fastest and most nimble know they won't be able to outrun their fates for long. It's heartbreaking. I see Nigel and his friend, the same as I did before. The two of them are running, then cowering. They're petrified. They're unlikely to survive.

"Why?" I ask again. "I wanted to warn them, but then Nigel hit me. Now, I'm here. Unable to do anything about this. It's Nigel's own fault. His hatefulness put me here."

Charmiene sends a puff of energy my way that wipes me clean, as if to say that I need to be more evolved, like she is. She has no patience for my squabble with Nigel or my interest in blaming him. I get it. I relax and try again.

"What can I do?" I ask. "I'd like to help. I always like to help."

She nods, then turns me once more. The scene sort of pans out, allowing me to see that it's on the mainland. The buildings are much taller than any we have on Hideaway Isle. It looks like downtown Miami. Yet, that doesn't make any sense. Nigel and his friend were here, on our island. How would they get to Miami, and why would I be seeing an explosion there? It feels outside the usual scope of my intuition. I study the black cloud more closely and decide that it is most definitely a larger scale tragedy than anything my intuition has let me be privy to in the past. This scene reminds me of old 9/11 footage we watched in history class. I'll never forget seeing the massive amount of smoke, dust, and debris pushing its way down the streets of Manhattan. And that was seeing it on TV. I can only imagine what that must have been like in person.

The terrorist attacks on September 11, 2001 changed America forever. I wasn't nearly old enough to grasp the enormity of what was happening at the time, but I think I get it now. Mrs. McClanahan lost a brother in the 9/11 attacks, and she told the students in her high school history class all about him and what he went through. His story made a big impression on me. It's interesting that Nigel was in that very same class, too. He heard the same stories I did.

Ross Anders was working on the eighty-seventh floor of tower two at the World Trade Center that fateful morning. He was an accountant at the New York State Department of Taxation and Finance. It was a good job, one that provided for his wife and two little kids. His wife was a stockbroker, but she wasn't working at that time because their kids were babies. Come to think of it, those kids are probably somewhere around my age. I guess I have something in common with them. We both lost our dads young. Funny how life weaves and connects, until it's one big web that we're all a small part of, stretching on for infinity.

Mrs. McClanahan recounted how she had talked to Ross that morning. For a while after the first plane hit, he had been alive and able to make phone calls. It hadn't been for long, though. If my memory serves me right, the first plane hit at 8:46 am. The building collapsed at 10:28. Don't ask me why I remember those exact times. Maybe it's because I'm in this otherworldly place right now. Maybe details of things I've seen and heard are heightened. Maybe I can access more information. Whatever the reason, I remember Mrs. McClanahan's description of the tearful conversation she'd had with her brother and how he knew he wasn't likely to survive. He had called the people closest to him to say goodbye. He and others trapped above the impact zone had been left with no possible way to escape. Stairwells and elevator shafts had all been destroyed or blocked.

As I look at the dramatic scene in the picture window, I can't help but wonder if I'm seeing something that will rival-- or surpass-- the worst terror attack in U.S. history. That's heavy. Tremendously so. I'm not sure what to do with that much information. If this event is destined to happen, I'm not sure I want to know about it. I'd like to help Nigel, but I just don't know what I can actually accomplish. This is huge. Way, way bigger than me. I'm just a small-town Wisconsin girl trying to live free and light on an island in the Florida Keys. It's enough work taking care of myself, not to mention using my artistic talents for portrait painting and my psychic abilities to give palm readings.

I don't want to be a hero. I just want to live my life. Live and let live, and all of that. If I can be with Lottie and I get a family as a bonus, then great. I know I'd step up for them. I already would for Lottie, Margot, Rags… even Puck and Chely. And Herbert. Hell, Chevelle, too. Basically, anyone important to Lottie is-- by extension-- important to me. Now that Lottie is back in touch with her sister and their newfound brother and grandpa, we're becoming a tight little group. I assume our circle will expand as time goes on. Maybe I really will get to be an aunt to Margot's kids. Or to Puck's kids, for that matter. He already has one on the way. And just maybe, Lottie and I will have kids of our own someday. That line of thinking is plenty heavy for me right now. The ideas of explosions and terrorist attacks are simply too much. Too massive. I'm powerless to stop them.

As far as I know, the best I can do in the face of impending terrorist attacks is to keep myself and my circle in a safe place, far away from the threat. And that might take some serious effort to accomplish. My intuition comes through as it pleases. I can't necessarily know everything I want to. I can't dial it up and make requests. Well, I guess I can make requests, but those requests aren't always granted. There's far more that I don't know as compared to what I do. Sometimes, my psychic abilities feel like a blessing and a curse. Ignorance might truly be bliss.

Charmiene seems to sense what I'm thinking. She waves a hand and the scene quickly rewinds. People on the street walk backwards, traffic is inverted, the smoke collapses in reverse from where it came, and soon there's nothing left but a bright, sunny Florida day. With the rewind complete, all is well. Gulls fly overhead and squawk merrily. Water in the Miami River sparkles, and a gentle breeze sways peacefully throughout the city.

Charmiene is showing me what happened before the explosion. This is definitely Miami. And the explosion is definitely something that hasn't happened yet.

"Okay," I say to let Charmiene know I'm following along. "What do you want me to see, specifically?"

She nods, realizing that I'm as ready as I'll ever be. The vantage point changes again. This time, there's a swoosh-like sensation and I can see the inside of a tall office building, presumably the one that will later explode and collapse. It looks like any other city office building, although I'm not sure I've ever been to such a building in person. My frame of reference is probably a product of things I've seen on television shows and movies. At any rate, the place looks standard. Rows of cubicles occupy a large open area in the middle of the space while offices with glass walls line the edges. Everything is fancy, polished to a high shine and immaculately clean. The place appears to be empty, which strikes me as curious. Maybe it's a weekend and the people who normally occupy this building are off work? Or maybe I'm not seeing the people yet, for some reason.

I glance back at Charmiene, unsure what it is she wants me to know. She prompts me to keep watching.

"Fine," I say, still impatient.

I want to get done with this so I can get back to my body and get on with my life. I don't mean to sound ungrateful. The time I've spent with Charmiene has already been life changing. How many people actually have a chance to communicate with their guardian angel? Or any angel, for that matter? But the fear of running out of time to return to the land of the living still nags me. I have physical recovering to do. I suspect that recovery won't be a small task. I anticipate a hospital stay, then rehab. It might be a while before I truly get back to normal. Or a new normal, at least.

"Watch," Charmiene prompts, more forcefully than before.

I'm alarmed by her insistence. And frankly, I'm scared about what I might see. I don't get the sense that I'm going to be in this office building if— or *when*— it explodes. I can't be certain, but it seems the threat is to someone besides me. I think Charmiene wants me to help thwart the attack, though. Maybe she's assigning me the task in exchange for going back to my body to survive for more years on Earth. Is it just Nigel and his friend? Or is there another connection?

I turn my full attention back to the gorgeous South Florida sunny day in the picture widow. I'm still inside the office building. Only this time, people begin to appear around me. I don't immediately recognize them. They're dressed up-- men in suits and ties and women in various put-together business attire. Their clothing and hairstyles look current, so I suppose this event is to take place relatively soon. Some of the people are sitting at desks, working away, oblivious to everything around them. Their voices rise and create a din that fills the background. It begins to drown out the celestial music from the sanctuary. I watch as the people go through motions that are probably routine for them, and it makes me think of Ross and what he must have been doing on the morning of 9/11. It pains me to realize that the people I'm seeing will apparently perish in a bombing, and they don't know what's coming. I look more closely at their faces. Their personalities seem to burst out the longer I study them.

Each of these people has loved ones. They're all special to someone. Husbands, wives, sons, daughters, parents, and friends. They all have dreams and plans for their futures. Many probably have kids waiting on them to return home and curl up on the couch at the end of the long day. Even pets will wait on their owners with fierce devotion. It's such a shame that a terrorist would mercilessly put an end to all of that love and beauty. I hate it. How could someone bomb a building full of innocent people? What motivation could possibly make the collateral damage worth it? I doubt I'll ever be able to understand the mind of a villain like that. I don't want to try.

"Okay," I say without shifting my attention. "This will be terrible if it happens. What can I do?"

My interest in helping is growing stronger, yet I still don't understand how I can assist. A disconnect remains. I'm not fully invested in getting the job done.

In a flash, Charmiene waves a hand again and the scene shifts. She shows me a dark room in the bowels of the building. It's steamy and sticky. A boiler room, maybe? Do they even have those anymore? Whatever this place is, it's ominous. Large pieces of equipment fill most of the space. An overhead light with a single white bulb flashes slowly over a large door bearing a row of chains and deadbolts. This room is quite a contrast to the shiny, clean offices I saw a moment ago. It's almost hard to believe it's the same building. Charmiene senses my doubt and adjusts the perspective once more, assuring me that we are, indeed, looking at the same building. I'm apprehensive, but I keep watching, scanning for clues and signs of trouble.

A long figure appears. It's crouching low to the floor.

Or maybe… Wait, it's coming into better view. It's sitting. The person— a woman— is sitting on a metal chair. But oh, no. She's restrained. There's a black gag cloth in her mouth that's wrapped around her head, tied tightly in the back. She's struggling furiously against bindings that keep her wrists and ankles attached to the chair. She looks at something on a card table nearby and I follow her gaze. I gasp when I see what she does. A huge bundle of wires and explosives sits just underneath the table, barely hidden from view. A timer attached to the front of the device counts down, presumably to detonation. It reads twenty-seven minutes.

Oh, my God. This poor woman knows it's coming. She's not oblivious like the others. She's been left here to watch the countdown to the end. Given the size of the explosives and the looks of the explosion as I've seen it, this woman will be blown to pieces the instant that thing detonates. I wonder what this unfortunate soul did to deserve this. Maybe she didn't do anything at all. Maybe she wound up at the wrong place at the wrong time, mixed up with the wrong people. How terribly sad for her.

Charmiene doesn't have to prompt me this time. I look more and more closely, drawn in by this woman's plight. My mind begins to strategize on how to help her. I want to help her. If there's anything I can do— anything at all— I'd like to do it. I focus on her face. Her cheeks shine as the flashing light illuminates her features. She's crying. Of course, she is. I don't blame her. I would be, too. She's young. She reminds me of…

"Oh, God…"

The young woman's features come into full view and

whatever heart I have at my current disposal stops beating.

It's Lottie.

The woman I'm seeing is my very own Lottie. How utterly devastating.

11

RUCKUS

I don't have time to blink. I'm pulled through time and space so hard it makes my head spin. In a dizzying whir of music and a haze of color, I'm sucked back into my body. I land with a thud, suddenly aware of every painful aspect of my physical presence. The discomfort is agonizing. It feels like I've been run over by a Mack truck, and my head is pounding like it's been on the receiving end of a jackhammer.

I hope this doesn't last long. I'm not sure how much I can endure. I've never experienced pain like this before. It's far more than what I felt when I broke my arm as a kid.

Ouch.

Surgery is finished. I'm in what appears to be a recovery room now. My eyes peek open and I can make out the black circular outline of a clock on the wall across from my bed. The hands go all wonky when I try to read them, though. It hurts to think. I scan my field of vision for anyone I can talk to. I've got to find Lottie. It's urgent.

I need to tell Margot, Rags, and the others what I saw while I was out of my body. The first step is finding a nurse or a doctor who will get them for me. Gingerly, I turn my head to one side. The pain catches and feels like a series of glass shards forcing their way through my flesh. Every twinge takes effort-- to move, to settle, and to bear the pain. How am I supposed to save Lottie when I'm so incapacitated? It doesn't add up.

I feel different. Not just physically. I feel *emotionally and spiritually* different. I've been changed.

I think what I just went through was a legitimate near-death experience. I'd heard of them. Aunt Portia had given me a few magazine articles to read which detailed first-person accounts of NDEs, as the scientists who study such phenomena like to call them. If I remember correctly, a decent percentage of the population has had a near-death experience. Something like three percent. Or maybe it's five. Whatever the exact number, it's more than most people probably assume it to be. All of a sudden, I want to get online and start reading other stories to see how they compare to mine. If I can't do that, then I'll go to a library and do the research the old-fashioned way. I'm eager to know I'm not alone. That what I just saw, heard, and felt wasn't a figment of my imagination. I believe it wasn't, but I seek solace in knowing that for sure.

"There she is," a young Asian nurse wearing a crisp white uniform says calmly. "Welcome back."

I can't see the details of her face yet. Everything is still fuzzy. She sounds nice, though. I'm glad to make human contact, back on this side of the veil. I try to nod, but pain grips me. I wince. My face scrunches up.

"Ow!" I mumble.

"Easy, Basia," she replies. "Let's take things slow."

"Okay," I say quietly, without moving another muscle. It hurts to talk, even just one word. It's less painful than turning my head, but not by much.

"I'm Ishi. Mrs. Ishi Moore, to be exact. I'll be taking care of you here in recovery."

"What about Agnes?" I ask.

Ishi smiles. I don't see it, but I feel it. My awareness is heightened even more than it used to be. It seems like my intuition has been amped up. I'm not sure how to use it yet, so I simply make a mental note and observe.

"Agnes Swanson?" she replies.

I don't dare nod again. Instead, I blink. Thankfully, Ishi sees it and gets the message.

"Agnes is a nurse on the neurology floor. Once you're stable and we're sure you no longer need intensive care, you'll go back there. You'll probably see her again."

That means they expect me to be in the hospital a while. I can read between the lines. If I could be discharged soon, Ishi would probably say something about how I might miss Agnes due to her regular days off each week. But she doesn't say anything of the sort. Just that I'll probably see Agnes again. I know this recovery won't be fast. One tiny movement and the resulting pain screams that fact loud and clear. I guess I'm hoping for a miracle. Is that too much to ask?

Charmiene didn't tell me a timeline for the Miami terror attack. For all I know, it could happen five years from now. Or ten. Or more. But I suppose it could go the other way, too. It could happen two weeks from now. Or two days. Or less. It feels urgent.

I have to stop myself there. That line of thinking won't give me anything except a clobbering dose of anxiety. And that won't help matters. I suppose I have no choice but to trust divine timing. If Charmiene thinks I can help circumvent the disaster, surely she knows that I'll have to recover first. I almost died. Or I guess... I actually did die. Regardless of the semantics, I'm not in any shape to hop out of bed and charge into the wider world right now. I'll have to proceed carefully. Without my physical strength, I won't be much help.

"Are you warm enough?" Ishi asks as she tucks blankets in around my arms and legs. "Sometimes, people are cold when they wake up from anesthesia. I can get more blankets if you need them."

I blink again, once for yes. I'm warm enough. Ishi gets it. She doesn't repeat the question.

"Too warm?" she tries.

I blink twice, and she moves on, notating my responses in what must be my chart. She holds a clipboard similar to the one Dr. Khatri had. She scribbles quickly with a silver pen. She has plastic gloves on, but they're thin enough that I can still feel her human touch as she lifts one of my wrists and takes my pulse. The hospital has machines for that, no doubt. Apparently, Ishi likes to do it the old-fashioned way. Maybe she likes to double check that the machines are accurate. I don't mind. Her touch is comforting. It anchors me, a counterbalance to the pain.

"I want to check your pain level, Basia, okay?" Ishi asks. "We want to keep you as comfortable as possible."

She holds up a chart with vertical numbers between zero and ten. Each number has a corresponding face ranging from a big, peaceful smile at zero to a twisted grimace at ten. Ishi points to five. It's a reasonable place to start, I suppose. I blink twice. No way is my pain level at a five. I raise my brows slightly, motioning her to move up the scale.

She notices and jumps to seven. I blink twice. Nope.

Eight? Nope. Blink twice.

Nine? I hesitate and consider my response. This pain sure feels like a ten, but it can always be worse, right? I decide nine is the best place to land for now, in case it gets worse. I blink once, slowly, hoping to communicate my unease about exactly where I fall at the top end of this scale.

How can I know what ten feels like? Is this it? Ishi probably knows better than I do. She tends to patients in my condition all the time, presumably.

"Nine it is. For now," she says as she scribbles the number in my chart. She glances at a smartwatch on her wrist, then up at the black-rimmed clock on the wall. "You can have more pain meds on the hour. Twenty-five more minutes."

That long? The disappointment is crushing.

I have big, important things to worry about. I have things to *do*. Being out of commission and forced to slow down to a crawl is so very frustrating. I want to jump out of this bed and race down the halls of this hospital until I find Margot and Rags. I want to force them to tell me where Lottie is. If they don't know, I want to hear everything they do know. I want Dr. Khatri to tell me why he acted cagey when I asked for Lottie to come into my room earlier. And I want to know why Agnes told me not to turn on the TV or access the internet on my mobile phone. What are they hiding from me? And why didn't Charmiene tell me more details about whatever it is that's happening with my own girlfriend? If Life is trying to teach me a lesson, it's really driving the point home. I wish this could be easier.

Tears stream down my face. I don't dare let myself heave. That would be far too painful. I close my eyes, trying hard to hold the emotion in. When I do, I see my dad. Visions of our time together in the heavenly garden come flooding back. It felt so good to hug him. To see his smiling face, full of love and concern for me. I've missed him so much. I didn't even realize how much. I wasn't aware of the full impact of the hole his absence had left in my life. I wish we'd had more time together here on Earth. I wish I'd known what had happened to him sooner. It would have saved me a lot of anger and resentment. It would have saved me from feeling like I wasn't good enough to stick around for. Life can be so cruel at times. So callous. And now, I'm hurting so badly, physically, that I want my parents. Both of them. I want Pa, and I want Mama. I want them here. Now.

Ishi notices my distress. She's carefully attuned, a good recovery room nurse. She puts a hand on my forearm and holds it there.

"I'm sorry, Basia," she says.

I can't be sure, but it seems like Ishi is apologizing for far more than the twenty-five minutes I'll have to wait for pain medication. I think she's sorry for everything I've gone through. For everything I've yet to go through. For the hard life that I've lived. Her compassion is genuine and palpable. She keeps her hand on me as the tears flow. I think about Nigel and how his hateful actions put me in this hospital bed. I think of Mama and how she doesn't even know what really happened to Pa. I think of Lottie and the various traumas she's endured. She lost Grandpa Vern only a few weeks ago. And I think about how I saw him. He looked well enough. Yet I was too preoccupied to communicate directly with him. I wonder if she'll be mad at me when she hears that I had a chance to ask him if he had a message for her but didn't do it. So many feelings lie tangled in my belly.

I blink once, thanking Ishi. I try to smile. I think the corners of my mouth turn up a little before the pain hits like a lightning bolt. I wince, thinking of Puck and the real lightning bolts that struck him, as well as the one that killed his, Lottie's, and Margot's grandma. It seems that every thought brings with it a fresh batch of remembered trauma and discontent. It's exhausting. And overwhelming. My pulse races, then I hear a beeping from a nearby monitor that keeps pace with my heartbeat. It goes so fast, so quickly, that Ishi has to respond. She steps away from my bed to grab something out of a cabinet, then she uses a needle and syringe and positions herself to add whatever it is into my IV. Probably a sedative. It's not good for me to be this worked up. I *know* that. I feel that. But I also don't want to spend any more time away from my body, or dreaming, or wherever else. If pain is my new reality, I can learn to cope with it. I need to stay alert and present. No sedatives.

I blink twice, forcefully, hoping Ishi notices before I have to speak. She does, and she pauses.

"Basia, it's important that we keep you calm. I can

give you something to make you sleep longer. It will settle your nerves until your body has had more time to heal."

I blink twice. "No," I say. "I have to stay awake. I..."

Before I can finish my sentence, a familiar voice sounds from across the room.

"Oh, good. She's awake?" Dr. Khatri asks.

I hear his feet shuffling as he makes his way to my bedside. He slows to a stop, and I see the outline of his figure. I squint to see the details, but they're fuzzy. He must notice my teary eyes because he puts a hand on my shoulder, the same as he did before my surgery.

"Basia, you did good, my friend," he says softly. "It was a tough surgery, but you came through with colors flying."

I chuckle. I don't think English is the doctor's first language. Mixing up the words as compared to the usual phrasing is probably due to his lack of familiarity with the English language. But it strikes me as appropriate since I literally saw colors flying around me as I descended from wherever my spirit was and reconnected with my body. His statement is spot on. I hurt too badly to explain, though.

"She's in a lot of pain," Ishi says to Dr. Khatri. "I was about to give her something to help her rest. I think she needs it."

Dr. Khatri takes my chart from Ishi and flips through a few pages. "Vitals look good," he says. "Are her pupils equal and reactive?"

"Yes," Ishi replies.

I don't remember her examining my pupils. There's so much I don't remember. Tears still pour from my eyes, and the incessant beeping continues to race with my heart. I silently wish for Dr. Khatri to help me. In fact, I *will* him to help me, using all my spiritual might. He stops what he's doing and stares at me hard. I blink once, hoping he gets the message.

"Basia, what can I do for you?" Dr. Khatri asks.

It's an unusual question, I think. He knows the recovery process. He ought to know better than I do what might help me. And besides, wouldn't that question make more sense coming from a nurse? Aren't doctors too busy to do the menial jobs that go along with a long, grueling recovery like the one I'm facing? Maybe my spiritual blast somehow made an impact.

I blink once, looking at Ishi.

"She's been blinking to communicate," she explains to the doc. "Once for yes…"

"Two for no. I understand," he confirms. "So, yes, you want me to do something for you?" he asks me.

I blink again. Once.

"Lottie?" I muster.

Dr. Khatri closes the chart and tucks the clipboard it's attached to under one arm.

"Who is Lottie?" Ishi asks.

"Her partner-- er, girlfriend-- I think," Dr. Khatri says. "She's been asking about Lottie ever since she woke up here in the hospital. Right, Basia?"

One blink. Yes.

"Please," I plead. "A visitor?"

It hurts so badly to talk. But if Lottie could walk through the door and kiss my tears, it would all be worth it.

Dr. Khatri hesitates and I can sense the same runaround coming that he tried to give me before surgery.

I'm sure he'll say I'm too weak. That I need to rest and recover. And plenty of other excuses to keep Lottie away. Or to keep me from knowing where she actually is.

"Soon," Ishi says. "As soon as you're stable, we'll get you to a regular room and your family can visit. Okay? You can help us speed up that process by staying calm."

"Don't…" Dr. Khatri begins. "She's been through enough. We almost lost her. She deserves to know more than what she's been told."

"Are you going to approve a visitor?" Ishi asks, clearly surprised. "Here, in recovery?"

"I don't know yet. Give me a minute to think," he replies. "It's all over the news, anyway. It's only a matter of time until someone tells her."

"Tells me what?" I ask.

My heart races even faster at the prospect of being given more information, and especially at the mention of something being on the news. Overwhelmed, I try to prop myself up in the bed. Pain hits me like a brick wall, knocking me down and out. I cry, a loud shriek that makes a nurse in an adjacent area poke her head in to see what's happening. My blood pressure spikes from the pain, and that monitor begins to alarm, sounding a cacophony with the heart rate monitor. The sound hurts my head. My movement hurts my head. Every damn thing hurts my head. It's misery.

"Basia, please, stay calm," Ishi pleads.

I don't listen to her. I'm too agitated. I'm suddenly like a wild animal, willing to fight against my captors with every ounce of strength I can muster. Common sense be damned.

"No!" I wail.

I flail in the bed, raising both arms to my head. I hold tightly to the soft bandage that's wrapped around my skull and carefully taped as I pull my knees to my chest and curl into a fetal position. In the process, the various tubes and cords attached to me get bound up. A blood oxygen monitor goes flying off my fingertip and wraps itself around a bed rail like seaweed on driftwood. The IV in my hand gets yanked, coming halfway out. It hurts, though not nearly as much as my head. A catheter that I had been previously unaware of tugs angrily between my legs as I twist in the bed. Compression machines wrapped around my calves come off in the struggle, and they, too, begin to alarm. Every sound and every physical obstacle pushes me further over the edge in my own mind.

I can't take this. I can't *do* this. It's too much. I don't have what it takes. I'm not cut out for this kind of adversity. I'm not strong enough. I just… I…

Out of the corner of my eye, I see Dr. Khatri preparing something in a fat syringe.

"No!" I say again. "N-O! No!"

I say the words as forcefully as I can. I mean for them to leave me alone. I want to get out of here. I need to get away. I…

I feel a prick on one side of my neck, then my vision gets really foggy. I turn to see Dr. Khatri, a look of solemn remorse on his face.

"I'm sorry, Basia," he says. "Get some rest. We'll watch over you."

Then, within seconds, everything goes black again.

I'm out once more. Down for the count.

12

DAYS GONE BY

For days-- I can't be sure how many-- I stay in the hospital, cycling in and out of consciousness. I don't see anyone but Ishi, Dr. Khatri, Dr. Marcellus, and a night nurse named Peg. I don't catch Peg's last name. I'm not sure it matters. Her job is a thankless one. I can only hope she does it out of the goodness of her heart and will forgive my inability to express my gratitude. These four people tend to me in my darkest hours. They fix and heal me with their medical expertise and their meticulous devotion to their protocols, checklists, and routines. They are a miracle of modern medicine. Any doubts I had about the qualifications of the staff at our island hospital vanish. They are quite literally some of the best, hands down. I'm lucky to have these fine people available to me. I'm lucky to be alive. But unfortunately, things get worse in my world before they get better.

Shortly after the injection in the neck, I'm placed on a ventilator for what I hear the doctor call airway protection. I do my best not to freak out from inside my prison of a damaged body, although it's incredibly hard. It feels like I'm suffocating as the tube is forced down my windpipe and my lungs are mechanically inflated. I want to scream from deep inside. I want to run away. Neither are possible. I'm fed liquid through a stomach tube several times a day. I'm not hungry. Not in the typical sense, anyway. My whole body feels different. Short circuited. The catheter takes care of waste disposal from my bladder. I don't have enough food in me to require use of a bedpan. At least, I'm not aware of it, if I am using a bed pan. I was thin to begin with. I suspect I'm losing a lot of weight that I don't have to spare.

My situation is precarious. I'm acutely aware of the danger, even though I'm not awake and conscious to talk about it. I may not know the details, but I'm certain this recovery will be hard won, if I ever get there.

The hours run together, a tangled mishmash of physical discomfort and emotional agony. It's so bad that I seriously consider going back to find Charmiene to tell her I've changed my mind. A part of me longs to see Pa and return to the garden, this time, to stay forever. It was so peaceful there. I desperately want some of that peace here in what has become a living hell on Earth. Pa could hug me again, and his love would help all this anguish fade away. I missed out on so many of his hugs growing up. It's very tempting to go with him now and bask in his attention for eternity. We have a lot of catching up to do.

I hear Dr. Khatri and Ishi talking about me. Something else went wrong. A complication with my recovery caused me to spend more time in the intensive care unit. My brain is still scrambled, and I can't make sense out of much of what they're saying. They mention surgery often. I think they want to take me back for another operation. Nothing would make me more upset than a second surgery. Another procedure would, no doubt, lengthen the time it takes me to heal and get back to some semblance of normal. I don't want to be delayed any more than is absolutely necessary. I pray hard that I won't need more surgery.

It feels like the Universe is conspiring against me. I need to get out of this place, yet I remain stuck here, facing what seem like endless obstacles. I felt so connected to loving beings during my near-death experience. Now, I feel distanced from everyone and everything. My intuition felt heightened during the experience and when I first woke up. Now, it seems like the switch has been shut off again. And again, I wonder what I did to deserve this. It feels so incredibly unfair.

I'm pinned between life and death, unable to move surely in either direction. As the misery wears on, I care less and less which path I take. I simply want a way out of this purgatory. I want an escape from the pain and isolation. Charmiene's state of being tempts me. She told me I had a choice. I frequently wonder if I made the wrong one. I wouldn't wish this on my worst enemy.

One day, I hit a metaphorical wall. At my wit's end, I decide that something has to give. In what I can only describe as a stern talking to myself, I force myself to choose… one final time. I tell myself to either get busy living or get busy dying. I know it sounds obvious, like a matter I should have tended to the minute I woke up from surgery. But it wasn't. And I didn't. I make up for lost time as best I can, though. I think of Lottie, and I reaffirm my decision to stay and live. She's worth any amount of suffering if it means I can save her and be with her. Besides, I want to be a part of the makeshift extended family group we have here on Hideaway Isle. And I want to see Mama and tell her about Pa. I'd decided all of this before, but apparently, I needed to reaffirm my choices to move forward.

With that settled once and for all, I turn my attention to what I *can* do rather than focusing on everything I can't. My consciousness is still intact, alive and well. Even if my brain is glitching here and there, I can use my consciousness to make plans. I begin going over everything I know that might be relevant to Lottie and the explosion scene I saw. Like Sherlock Holmes examining clues, I use all my intelligence to sort through bits and pieces of information. The concept of time and space remains warped, but it feels like a long time that I spend on this mental task. I work on it as long as I can, then I rest until I have enough energy restored to go at it again.

I remember hearing about a paralyzed man who did something similar. Aunt Portia told me the story when she was teaching me about intuition and psychic abilities. I guess she wanted me to understand the power of the human mind to overcome adversity. She said that the man had been in a bad car accident. The bones in his legs were shattered, and doctors didn't think he could possibly walk again. He'd had a head injury, too, and he was mostly out of it, like me. And like me, he heard doctors talking about him. In fact, I'm pretty sure they thought he was a goner. But the man didn't let that stop him. He decided he was going to prove them wrong and walk out of that hospital on his own two legs one day, no matter how long it took. As he lay incapacitated, he used his mind to rehearse his comeback. He worked hard to remember the fine movements involved with walking, then he visualized himself making those movements over and over and over again. He got down to the nitty gritty with each muscle needed to make a person walk upright with enough balance to keep going. And you know what? That man's recovery took a long while, but he ultimately did leave that hospital walking on his own two feet. I was inspired by the story when I first heard it. Little did I know what a lifeline it would offer me now.

I decide if that man can do it, so can I. My challenge is greater because I not only have to get myself well enough to get out of here, but I have to put together clues and solve the mystery of how to save Lottie from certain death at the hands of terrorists. Not to mention, I've got to save all of those other innocent people who will be killed if the bomb I saw goes off. The stakes are too high for me to wimp out and give up. I decide to give it my all.

So, I do just that. I wade through the uncertainty and I keep my mind at work. Eventually, I piece together a collection of facts that might be relevant. Facts related to the accident that happened with Lottie's boat tour company, to her grandfather's murder, and to the day she and I were held hostage by Llew Brackus and his goons. There are so many possibilities related to all of that. The current situation and my premonition might be completely separate, but that seems unlikely the more I consider it all. If I had to guess, this new threat has something to do with the events of late. Nigel and his friend don't quite fit in with that theory. Maybe they're just in the wrong place at the wrong time. Or maybe they will get involved in a future that hasn't yet come to pass.

Either way, by the blessed morning I finally wake up having recovered enough to get the ventilator removed, I have a solid grasp of the background information needed to solve the mystery and thwart the attack, all stored in my hard-working mind.

I'm proud of myself. I did the mental work, and hopefully, I'll reap the rewards.

I recover quite suddenly. It seems sudden, anyway. One day I'm delirious, and the next I'm waking up, feeling strong and alert.

"Look at you go, girl," Ishi says to me with a smile as she slowly removes the tube from my throat, then gently wipes the spittle from the corners of my mouth. "You're a tough cookie, Basia Guthrie. One of the toughest I've seen."

I cough and gag. It takes a few minutes to find my bearings again now that my airway is left to function on its own. My strength is returning at what feels like a remarkable pace, but I'm still weak.

"Thank you," I squeak out. My first words in quite some time feel amazing rolling off my tongue. "Lottie?" I ask. I can't waste any time waiting to ask about her.

Ishi smiles sadly now, her gloved hands busy bunching up the tube that just came out of my throat. She glances toward the door, apparently looking to see if anyone else is listening. Maybe she wants Dr. Khatri to be the one to tell me whatever it is they have to say.

"She's not here, hon," Ishi says when she confirms the coast is clear. "I'm sorry."

I nod, surprised that my head isn't pounding when I do. I really have gotten better. I wonder how long I've been intubated.

"Visitors?" I ask.

I'd love to see Margot and Rags. Or anyone, really. I'm desperate for human interaction with those of the living, breathing variety.

Ishi raises and lowers her brows several times, her whole face animated. "Now, that I can help you with," she confirms. "As soon as Dr. Khatri comes by to examine you, we'll get you transferred to a regular room. And there, you can have visitors! Two at a time, for as long as you want until eight o'clock this evening."

Ishi does a little dance after she says it, lifting her elbows and moving her hips from side to side. I appreciate her enthusiasm. It makes me smile to match her expression. Her energy is contagious. Thank God and everything holy. It feels so good to be smiling again.

"Good," I say.

There's a moment of silence between us while I consider what I should ask. I assume Ishi is letting me set the pace. She watches me out of the corner of her eye as she checks my vitals and makes notes in my chart.

"Hungry?" she asks.

Instinctively, I reach for the feeding tube that goes into my abdomen. "Can I eat?" I ask.

Ishi chuckles. "We won't bring you sausage and eggs just yet, but you can have clear liquids. The muscles in your mouth and throat need to wake back up and learn how to function normally again."

"What do you mean by that?" I ask. My voice is shaky.

"When your breathing is assisted by a machine like yours was, the muscles in your throat and esophagus are immobilized. Those muscles atrophy, which means they get smaller and weaker. They'll come back, though. They just need to do their thing and practice. We'll start with some chicken broth and see how it goes. How does that sound?"

I contemplate her explanation. I have a lot of questions. I do feel hungry, though. Chicken broth sounds surprisingly appetizing right now. I nod.

"I'd like the broth," I say.

"Good choice," Ishi confirms. "I'll have some delicious broth warmed and brought in. Guaranteed to be the best you've ever tasted!"

"Really?" I ask.

"After what you've been through? Really," she says.

Ishi is bobbing around the room making various preparations when Dr. Khatri walks in. He pauses to knock gently on the open door as a formality. I look over at him and am thrilled that my head doesn't throb when I do.

"Come in," Ishi says. "We've been waiting for you."

13

BOGEY

I smile. “Hi,” I say shyly.

A flash of the view from my near-death experience comes to mind when I see his face. I’ll probably never forget what I saw as I floated above my body. I’ll never forget seeing the top of Dr. Khatri’s head, his entire body steeped in concentration as he gave it his all to save me. He and Dr. Marcellus-- along with the nurses and aids who assist them-- are angels right here on Earth. How could I ever repay him?

“Hello, Basia,” the doctor says, taking a dollop of hand sanitizer and spreading it over his hands in what has now become a familiar method. “I’m pleased to see you awake and recovering so well.”

I nod. I’m not sure what to say. Their reactions tell me that I was in pretty bad shape. They seem almost surprised that I’m alive. Surprised that I made it. If I didn’t know better, I’d think they had written me off as a goner. Did they?

“Thank you,” I reply in a small voice.

"How are you feeling?" Dr. Khatri asks as he sits down on a rolling stool next to my bed. Ishi hovers in the background, ready to hand him anything he may need.

"My throat is sore," I say.

"That's to be expected," he confirms. "It's an unfortunate side effect of being on a ventilator. The feeling will go away in a few days. We can get you an oral antiseptic that will help."

He gestures to Ishi as he says it. She scribbles his order down.

"There's a pharmacy right here in the hospital," she adds. "It won't take long."

Dr. Khatri moves to pull my eyelid down, then pulls a small light the shape of a pen out of the pocket of his lab coat. He shines the light in one of my eyes, then the next, watching carefully as he does.

"Reaction is good," he says under his breath to Ishi, who scribbles some more.

"Got it," she confirms.

"How's your head? Any pain?" he asks me.

He doesn't touch my head. Maybe touching it wouldn't tell him anything, anyway. The problem was internal.

"Good," I say, reaching up to feel it where I remember it hurting. The area is still bandaged. "It doesn't hurt anymore. At least, not like it did. I mean… so far, it doesn't hurt. I haven't tried to move much yet..."

I'm rambling. I tell myself that's okay. I have every right to ramble. Every right to still be out of sorts. This is a marathon, not a sprint.

"That's very good," Dr. Khatri says.

He shifts his weight back on the stool, assessing my

frame of mind. I can tell he has a lot to say. He's measuring his words, taking it slow. I just hope we don't run out of time to get everything out in the open like we did before I was rushed into surgery. It seems calmer now. Like we can talk at length, if my shaky vocal cords are up to the task.

"Where's Lottie?" I try.

Dr. Khatri purses his lips. "I honestly don't know, Basia. I realize you're very concerned about her. If I knew where she was, I'd tell you. I swear."

Tears well up in my eyes, but I push them back. There will be time to be emotional later. I need to spend this conversation learning as much as possible while I have the doctor's full attention. Ishi stands at the ready behind him. She seems to sense that this conversation may take a while. She sets the clipboard with my chart down on a counter, then leans her weight back against it. In the intensive care unit, I presume this is as casual as it gets.

"What happened to me?" I ask. "After… I… I was awake before."

"When we performed your craniotomy surgery, we had to cut a portion of your skull out and make a flap to access the subdural haematoma," Dr. Khatri explains matter-of-factly. "That flap got infected, which caused further complications."

I jerk my hand up to feel the bandaged part of my head again. I don't understand all of the terms Dr. Khatri is using, but I get the gist of it. The thought of a flap being cut in my skull is unnerving. Ishi can apparently tell what I'm thinking.

"It's a temporary flap," she adds. "The section of your skull that was temporarily removed was then put back in place and secured using metal plates and screws. Right, Doctor?"

Dr. Khatri nods. "That's right. Infection of the wound is a common complication. Brain surgery is hard on the body…"

I take a deep breath as I try to absorb this news. My lungs catch when I do. They're still weak. I knew it was bad, but I didn't imagine a flap being cut out of my skull and then screwed back in like a puzzle piece.

"So, the infection was severe?" I ask.

"It was," Dr. Khatri continues. "You became septic. Sepsis is when an infection moves to your blood. People with brain injuries are particularly susceptible to sepsis. And that kind of systemic infection exacerbates the body's inflammatory response and leads to organ dysfunction."

I squint, mentally dissecting the words I can make sense of.

"My organs had trouble?"

"Yes, they had begun to fail," he confirms. "It was touch and go for several days. Your recovery is really quite remarkable."

There's a glimmer in Dr. Khatri's eyes as he says this, as if I'm a science experiment he can't wait to present to his nerdy friends. I guess I don't blame him. I choose my questions carefully, hoping to understand.

"You said several days?" I try.

"Yes, that's right."

"How long have I been here?" I ask.

Dr. Khatri glances at Ishi, who gives him a look that seems to say he should proceed with care. The doc is great, but Ishi seems better at comforting patients and not giving them more information than they can handle.

Don't get me wrong, I want the information, but it's increasingly hard to handle. I guess my mind protected me from all of this while I was floating around Charmiene's sanctuary and garden. Reality is a hard pill to swallow.

"Six days," Dr. Khatri says softly.

I'm shocked by this number. "*Six*?" I ask. "But that's almost a week."

He nods. "You were admitted on the twenty-first," he explains, checking his smartwatch to be sure the dates match up. "It's the twenty-seventh."

"Of June," Ishi adds. "Still June."

I suppose that much is good. It would add an extra layer of weirdness to this if a new month had rolled over without me knowing. But six days is a long time. On one hand, it feels like more than six days. I wouldn't have been totally shocked if Dr. Khatri had said I'd been in this hospital for months. But on the other, it feels like I just got here. A lot can happen in six days. I wonder what this means for Lottie. Why isn't she here? I still can't make any sense out of her absence.

"Okay," I say, resigned to the truth. "Six whole days."

Dr. Khatri nods, waiting for my next question.

"Margot… Did she…?"

"Margot acted as your decision maker, per your instructions," he confirms. "She gave us permission to put you on a ventilator. I hope you're pleased with that choice. Some patients don't want extraordinary measures or artificial sustenance of life, but without that ventilator, I assure you, you wouldn't be here right now."

I nod quickly, agreeing completely with Margot's

brave decision. I want to be here. I'm glad she made sure that the correct decision was made.

"That's good," I say. "I'm glad."

I reach a hand up and touch the outside of my throat. It may be sore, but it's sore for good reason. Suddenly, I become aware of the catheter between my legs. I reach down and pull at it, finding that it won't budge.

"We can take that out now," Dr. Khatri says to Ishi.

She moves quickly to the other side of my bed and lifts the tube that connects my bladder to a bag of urine hung nearby. She flips a switch on the tube and the balloon inside of my bladder deflates. Within minutes, Ishi pulls the catheter out. The reprieve is huge. My whole body breathes a sigh of relief.

"Thank you," I say.

I'm so grateful for every little thing now that I'm a survivor.

"Better?" Ishi asks with a smile.

"Much," I say.

Dr. Khatri smiles approvingly as Ishi folds up the catheter, then scribbles more notes in my chart. We watch her silently. We don't speak again until she's done and leaning against the counter, ready to converse with us. I break the silence.

"Ishi says I can go to a regular room now? And have visitors."

"You can," the doc replies. "But Basia, you aren't ready to leave the hospital yet. You'll need to stay at least a couple more days."

"Okay," I say. "I don't feel well enough to leave yet, anyway. I'm not strong enough."

"I'm glad to hear that you realize that," Dr. Khatri

says. "But Basia, you're going to learn things soon that will make you want to get right out of bed so you can get in the middle of them. Don't do it."

I look at him quizzically. I'm so sick and tired of people alluding to these unspecified things that I either can't know or will have a hard time taking when I do. What gives? I want the truth. It made be hard to take, like the details of my injury and illness were, but there are certain things I must know.

"Like what things?" I ask. "What will I learn?"

Dr. Khatri and Ishi glance at each other, in cahoots.

"For starters," he says, "a detective from the Hideaway Isle Police Department wants to question you. Tom Marsh."

I snap my head quickly, surprised. Now the pain hits me. It feels like someone is driving a nail straight into my skull.

"Ouch," I say.

"Easy," Ishi replies. "You may feel a lot better, Basia, but you're not back to one hundred percent yet. Take it slow."

I nod very slowly. "I know. You're right. I just… the police?"

"Yes," Dr. Khatri says. "I'm not privy to the details, but the man who injured you has been arrested and charged."

"Nigel?" I ask.

I guess I should have known that he would be. For some reason, that likely turn of events slipped my mind. Or maybe I thought it would be up to me. Like on TV, I suppose I thought someone would come to me and ask me if I wanted to press charges. I have half a mind to let

Nigel off the hook. It feels somehow wrong to send him to jail or prison or wherever for years when it might have been an accident. Maybe he didn't mean to injure me so badly. He certainly couldn't have known that I'd need surgery, or that my wound would get infected and I'd become septic. I highly doubt he had any idea. Hell, he might not have even expected me to turn like I did at the last minute. He might have been aiming for Lottie. The thought makes my blood boil. If he had been aiming for Lottie, I'd want to press charges. Perhaps I should be as protective of myself.

"Yes," the doctor confirms. "As he should be. You almost died. And then he would have been facing a murder charge."

The emotional impact of this statement hits me hard. I hadn't thought of it that way. Wow. Nigel nearly *murdered* me. Murder is a serious, scary word. What happened to me doesn't feel that serious or that scary, but I guess it is.

"Gosh," I say, lowering my voice. "I hadn't thought about it like that."

"That's understandable," Dr. Khatri says. "But after what he did to you, that young man deserves to be punished. I encourage you to start thinking about it like that. He's a threat to your safety and to the safety of others."

"You're right," I say. "Something should be done to keep him from hurting anyone else."

"That's exactly what Detective Marsh intends to do. I hope you'll cooperate with him. Tell him everything you know."

Dr. Khatri puts a hand over his mouth when he finishes, as if maybe he shouldn't have said so much. I'm glad he did, though. I don't have parents to guide me through this. I'm not sure of all the right things to do. I appreciate all the advice I can garner from the older, smarter people I trust. And I do trust Dr. Khatri. With my life, obviously. He already saved it once.

"I will," I confirm.

After a breath, the doctor continues.

"I want you to begin thinking about your discharge from the hospital," he says. "You're going to need someone with you at all times for at least the first few days. I'd feel better if someone was with you for several weeks. By the time we discharge you, the chance will be small, but you could still have another brain bleed. Or another infection. You need someone with you who can notice any changes to your behavior that could signal trouble. I can't stress how important this is, Basia."

"Okay," I say, thinking about what I'll do if Lottie isn't available.

"Margot tells me that you live in an RV with your girlfriend. Is that correct?"

"Yes," I reply.

I'd forgotten all about my RV. It doesn't seem like the best place to recuperate, but it's all I have.

"Is there someplace else you can stay for a while?" Dr. Khatri asks. "Somewhere with more room to move around and an easier time of cooking and bathrooming would be a good idea. Just until you're healed."

I wrack my brain as I think about who I might stay with. I'm not sure Dr. Khatri realizes what a loner I am. I don't have another place to go. Not really. I'm doing well to afford the RV, which reminds me. I need to make a payment to the campground so they don't have my RV towed. It was due a few days ago. On the twenty-fifth of every month. Panic seizes me. I sit up straighter in the bed.

"They might have towed the RV," I say. "Payment was due. I've… I've been here. I don't have any idea if Lottie or Margot knew to pay the campground. I need to talk to one of them." I ruminate on all that I need to sort out. "Lottie has a condo I could normally stay at, but we'd been avoiding it ever since her Grandpa Vern was killed and Llew and his guys held us hostage at Heron Cottage. I'm not sure what's happening with either place. I'm not sure what's happening with *Lottie…*"

Dr. Khatri and Ishi's eyes widen. That was a lot. I should slow down. I press my lips together, stopping the words that want to come out. I don't want them to sedate me again. They're right. I need to take it easy. I can't solve all of my problems at once. I need to focus on getting better.

"That sounds upsetting," Dr. Khatri says. "I knew you had a lot on your plate, but I didn't realize it was all of that."

"I'm so sorry," Ishi says. "I wish I could fix it for you."

I appreciate the sentiment. I wish she could fix it, too.

"I'll figure it out," I say. "Now, please. Tell me what you know about Lottie. Something is wrong, or she'd be here. I'm gaining strength. I can take whatever it is. Just tell me the truth."

They exchange knowing glances once more.

Dammit.

"Okay, Basia," Dr. Khatri says. "You're an adult, you're recovering from your injury, and despite our desire to protect you, you have a right to know. You *deserve* to know."

"Thank you," I say, most sincerely. I wad up the blanket over my chest and hold onto it tightly. I need something physical to anchor me. "Go ahead."

After a breath, Dr. Khatri begins. He looks pained as he does. The man clearly doesn't want to tell me anything upsetting. But he says the words anyway.

"Basia, your girlfriend, Lottie, has gone missing."

"What? How can that be?" I ask. "She's a grown woman, not a child. Who would take her?"

"I didn't say she was taken," he clarifies. "I said she'd gone missing. They don't know what happened. She's been gone ever since the day you were injured. She might have left of her own volition."

"Who is they?" I ask, desperately.

The fiery scene from the explosion fills my mind's eye. Lottie had been tied up in the room with the bomb. She had presumably been taken in order to have wound up in that spot. It isn't like she'd tie herself up. My heart races as I contemplate the implications of this news.

"The police. Also, Margot and Rags. No one has heard from Lottie. A lot of people are looking for her. Using all of the resources at their disposal."

Tears fill my eyes as my own helplessness hits me like a slap in the face. I want to rage against the powers that be. To question Charmiene. Why would she send me back into such an impossible situation? Before I can get too worked up, I talk myself down. I remind myself that I've done the mental work to help solve this mystery. I have to trust my ability to help. As my panic subsides, I'm comforted by the fact that there's a good reason for

Lottie's absence. If she had chosen to stay away from the hospital all this time, it would have hurt me badly. Now, I know for sure that she couldn't be here. That's but a small comfort, though it helps a little.

I begin to think pragmatically.

"Who can I see when I get to the regular room besides Detective Marsh?" I ask. "Margot? I need to talk to her."

14

RIDDLE ME

It takes another few hours before I'm moved out of intensive care and into a regular room. I spend a portion of that time napping while I wait for the head nurse on the neurology floor to call Ishi and let her know they're ready for me. I'm still gaining strength, after all. I eat some broth, which tastes every bit as good as Ishi promised it would. By the time I'm wheeled down to my new digs, I feel prepared for rapid progress.

A young man from patient transport pushes my bed down the hall, then up the elevator a few floors. I had sort of hoped to get out of the bed and into a wheelchair, but I'll take the victories as they come. I'm happy with my improvement.

I think Ishi may have pulled some strings because she told me that she thinks Agnes will be my day nurse here on the neurology floor. I can hardly contain my smile as I approach the door to my new room and I see Agnes' name written on a whiteboard above the room number. I can't wait to see her.

"Yes!" I say when I see it.

The patient transport guy chuckles, then opens the door to my room and wheels me in. To my surprise, I already have visitors. Puck and Herbert sit in a pair of chairs near the window, waiting eagerly for me. Their faces light up when their eyes meet mine.

"Basia! You're here," Puck says as he stands to greet me.

As soon as the wheels on my bed are locked in place and the transport guy takes his leave, Puck walks over and takes my hand. I'm thrilled to see him.

Puck Reed is sort of a dorky guy. He's often awkward in social situations. At least, he is compared to smooth and self-assured Rags. Lottie and Margot have already embraced Puck as their brother, though, so I will, too, by extension. Maybe all big brothers should seem a little dorky, right? I've never had one, so I don't really know. What I do know is that I so appreciate Puck and Herbert showing up for me.

"I am!" I reply. "Finally. Thanks for coming to visit."

"Of course," Puck says. "Happy to be here."

Puck smiles his sweet, sheepish smile, and I could kiss the guy. It really is so nice of him to come.

"Hello, dear," Herbert says with a wave when I glance his way.

He has one leg crossed over the other at the knee. He doesn't get up. I don't blame him. He's older and probably tired from waiting around. There's no need for him to get up to greet me.

"Hi, there," I say, "Mr. Finley."

I'm unsure what to call Herbert. He's Lottie's grandpa-- her mom's dad. She didn't know he existed until a couple weeks ago, though. Last I heard, she hadn't quite decided what to call him either. Maybe Grandpa Finley or Grandpa Herbert. I suppose I could call him one of the same, if he doesn't mind. I'd like to feel like I have family around. He takes the lead.

"Please, call me Grandpa," he says with a wink. "If you're with Lottie, you're with all of us. You're family."

I'm deeply touched by his words. To come from a place of not being accepted for my sexual orientation to being welcomed into a family before Lottie and I are even married means the world to me.

"Okay," I say gratefully. "Should I call you Grandpa Herbert? Or Grandpa Finley?"

"Whatever your pleasure," he replies with a grin.

Herbert is a dapper old gentleman. He's from a time when men were honorable in a way that brings a tear to my eyes. My admiration for men of his generation is probably due to not knowing the Guthrie men as anything other than abandoners. I realize now how wrong I was about Pa, but it doesn't change the fondness I've developed over the years for old gents like Herbert.

"I'm not sure what Lottie would want," I say, the energy in the room growing heavy at the repeated mention of her name.

"I'm not sure, either," Puck adds. "Margot and Lottie called their other grandfather Grandpa Vern. Vernon was his first name. Seems like Grandpa Herbert would be the way to go. You know? Keeping the first name in the name and all."

"Good point," I say, squeezing Puck's hand. "Grandpa Herbert it is."

Herbert likes the sound of that. He winks and nods at the same time. If he had a top hat, I'm sure he'd tip it.

We all look at each other for a moment, unsure of what to say or do next. I have a ton of questions, but I don't know Puck or Herbert nearly as well as I've come to know Margot and Rags. I want to take it slow. Thankfully, Herbert is the type of man you can be with and don't even have to worry about making conversation. Puck told me that about him, and he's right. We can sit together in silence, if we so choose.

"Hey," Puck says. "Do you feel up to a little music?"

"Sure," I reply, surprised. "Music might help lift my spirits."

"Nice!" he says, dropping my hand and walking over to retrieve something out of a backpack that sits tucked under his chair. "Sit tight."

I use the remote to raise the head of my bed, hoping to get a better view. To my delight, Puck pulls out three pair of sunglasses, a stuffed parrot, and a wide-brimmed straw hat. He puts the hat on my head, the parrot on my lap, and a pair of sunglasses on each of us. Then he cues up a music app on his smartphone and plays *Margaritaville*. It's the live version-- my favorite.

"Aw," I say, so touched I might devolve into a puddle of tears. "This is so sweet, Puck. How did you know I liked Jimmy Buffet?"

"Margot told me. Lottie told her."

"It's nice of you-- and Margot-- to pay attention," I say. "It means a lot to me."

"I'm glad," Puck says.

I'm struck by his sincerity. I knew he was a good guy, but it wasn't until this very moment that I realized the depth of that goodness. There's something about him that reminds me a lot of Lottie. An intangible quality that's hard to describe. They both just make you feel like you're safe with them. Margot, too, for that matter. The Reed-Callaway siblings are good eggs. Their mother, Annie, must have done something right.

Jimmy's iconic voice fills the room, singing about sponge cake, shrimp, and his lost shaker of salt. The familiar sounds of the steel drums and acoustic guitars wash over me, lifting my spirits like nothing else could. Puck adjusts the straw hat on my head, tipping it forward, careful not to interfere with my bandage. He's a good caretaker, tending to me with love. I lean back and close my eyes, bringing forth a relaxing beach scene from one of my favorite spots on Hideaway Isle. I've spent countless hours on that beach, in that very spot. I can recall the details vividly.

In this vision, I'm wearing my favorite black bikini. The one I bought at a little bohemian-vibe shop downtown when I first moved to the island. It's a simple design-- nothing noteworthy-- but it fits well, and stays put when I swim in the ocean. It looks good enough on me. I've been told it accentuates my muscular physique. At this point, after several years living on the island, that black bikini feels as comfortable and homey as my favorite pair of fuzzy slippers did back in Wisconsin. It's sort of my uniform. When I'm not working or hanging out at the campground, I'm usually at the beach.

As I submit myself fully to the experience and visualize myself on my favorite beach, every one of my senses comes into sharp focus. I can feel the smooth sand beneath me. It's packed tightly enough to support my weight, yet it gives as my cupped hands move it to and fro at my sides. I hear the ocean in the distance. Waves shift and crash effortlessly against the shore in their dance as old as time. The sound soothes me. Combined with Jimmy's rousing Margaritaville, it's the perfect soundtrack to a blissful existence. One that surpasses the wildest dreams I had before I moved south. And the smell… Oh, the smell of the sea. It's like nothing else.

I take all the sensory input from my memories and visions, and I pack it up and hold it tight against my very soul. Then, to connect all that goodness to the here and now, I imagine myself wearing the hat Puck has given me while on the beach, just like I am here in this hospital bed. One day soon, I'll be back on that beach. When I get there, I'm taking this hat with me. I'm going to lounge in the sand and bask in the sun. I'll play Margaritaville and smell the sea. It will be glorious. Absolutely glorious.

I hear the sound of shades being opened in my hospital room, so I open my eyes. Puck has pulled the curtain back and is fiddling with the tie. I squint against the sunlight, using my new hat to shield my eyes until they're used to the brightness.

"Oh, sorry," Puck says. "I didn't mean to disturb you. You looked so peaceful. I thought I'd let some light in. It's a beautiful day out there. I wasn't sure if you knew."

"It's okay," I say. "You're sweet."

I hate to call Puck sweet, but it's the most accurate description. He has an innocence about him that I find rare and special. He blushes at the compliment.

"Thanks, I guess," he says.

"You're exactly right," I confirm. "I had no idea what a beautiful day it was outside. There wasn't a window on the wall in my intensive care room. Maybe they need the wall space for equipment. Or maybe ICU patients aren't awake long enough to appreciate a window. Whatever the reason, I've been sun deprived. You've saved me!"

"That makes sense," Puck replies. "The thing about those patients not being awake long enough. I guess you did a lot of sleeping while you were in there."

"You can say that again. I almost fainted when they told me I've been here for six days. It felt like less."

"I get it," Puck confirms.

Herbert nods from the back of the room, and my attention shifts to him. He has a newspaper stretched between his hands-- the Miami Herald. He must have pulled it out while I was imagining myself on the beach. Seeing Miami on the front page makes my mind perk up and move into high gear. I had planned to ask for my laptop, but a newspaper is a good place to start. Especially one from Miami. I have investigating to do.

The song on Puck's playlist changes and Jimmy Buffet kicks off *Changes in Latitudes, Changes in Attitudes*. I love all of Jimmy's songs, but this one is probably in my top three, along with *Margaritaville* and *Cheeseburger in Paradise*. If Puck chose this order, he did a bang-up job. I enjoy hearing the music more than Puck knows. But I want to get my hands on that newspaper.

"Grandpa Herbert?" I ask, trying the name out.

"Yes, dear?" he replies, not skipping a beat. He seems comfortable with me addressing him that way.

"Could I take a look at that newspaper?"

I suddenly remember that Tom Marsh is supposed to come talk to me. I don't want to run out of time to garner all the information I can from Puck and Grandpa Herbert before Tom gets here.

Herbert shrugs. "Sure. I can get another one on my way out. Here, take it," he says as he folds it up and hoists it in my direction.

Puck scurries over to take the newspaper from his grandfather, then hands it to me.

"Whatcha looking for?" Puck asks.

It's an interesting question. I didn't say I was looking for anything in particular. I might have wanted to do some light reading, for all Puck knew. Unless he thinks there's something I should see. His statement piques my curiosity.

"I'm not sure," I say. "But I'll know it when I see it."

He lowers his brow and seems interested. "Can I help somehow?"

"Actually, yeah," I say. "You can help a lot, if you're up for it."

"I definitely am!" Puck exclaims excitedly.

Herbert chuckles from his chair but doesn't get involved in the conversation. Instead, he just listens. He strikes me as a guy who takes that approach to life, in general. He must learn a lot that way. I focus my attention on Puck and our budding partnership. Perhaps we can work together. Maybe he can be my confidante. The guy I bounce ideas off. He seems eager to do right by the Callaways. Maybe he'll get his chance.

"Look," I say, "I have a lot to figure out. I know Lottie's missing. And I know that a detective from the local police department is coming to talk to me. I could use a partner to help me solve some of the mystery surrounding all of this. Just maybe, you and I would make a good team. We're both sort of outsiders, new to the family, yet we care very much."

"Right. I see," he muses. "Okay, then. Where do we begin?"

I place my new hat on the stand beside me, then raise the upper portion of my mechanical bed to a sitting position.

"Do you know where my big blue bag is?" I ask. "I had it with me at the restaurant when…"

"When you were injured?"

"Yeah."

Puck crumples his face as he thinks. "I'm not sure. Margot didn't mention it."

"My laptop was in there," I say. "I could really use that to do some internet research."

"Of course," Puck replies. "I'll go find your nurse and ask. Okay? Then we'll get down to business. You can tell me what you need, and I'll help you find whatever you want to know."

PART III

HAZE

15

SEEK AND FIND

Herbert excuses himself to take a walk, claiming his old bones can't sit still for too long or they freeze up on him. He says it will give Puck and me some time to hash out our master plan. He kisses me on the forehead when he leaves, as if it's the most natural thing in the world. He gives me grandfatherly vibes, and I love it. I didn't even know I needed a grandfather in my life, but it turns out that I do.

Puck returns from the nurse's station with the news that Margot and Rags have taken my personal belongings home with them. That makes sense. No one knew when-- or if-- I'd wake up. I don't blame them. Puck promises to get my bag, laptop, and phone back here as soon as possible. But we don't have to wait to get started on our investigative work. Puck has a smartphone. And he has a large sketchpad in his Jeep. I flip through the newspaper while he goes downstairs to get the sketchpad. I don't ask where Margot and Rags are. I get the idea Puck doesn't know, exactly. We'll get to that. I can only assume they're out looking for Lottie, as they should be.

Before I can get too far into the newspaper, a male nurse comes in to check on me. I'm sad that he isn't Agnes, but my mood lightens when I hear that she'll be taking care of me just as soon as shift change happens, scheduled within the hour. That's fantastic news. I cooperate as the man checks my vitals and makes notes in my chart. That chart must be getting mighty lengthy by now. So many notes. So many checks. When he's satisfied that I'm in decent shape, he leaves me be.

I really am in decent shape. My vision isn't blurry anymore. My head doesn't hurt as long as I move slowly. I can read the newspaper clearly. The sun beams coming in from the window feel good on my skin. Whether I should attribute my rapid improvement to a miracle or simply the way recovery usually works, I don't know. It doesn't matter, at the end of the day, I suppose. I'm just glad it's happening. I'm glad I'm getting better.

"Found it," Puck says as he returns and slides in through the partially open door.

He sort of reminds me of a thirty-something skater dude with those moves.

I'm alone in the room, waiting for him, when he arrives. He holds the sketchpad under one arm. He wasn't kidding. It's big. The sketchpad has a hard back on it that functions like a tabletop for support. The sight of its wide-open blank pages do my heart good. I hadn't thought about it since being admitted to the hospital, but I've really missed painting portraits. Art is an important part of who I am. I'm drawn to it. Especially illustration. In fact, I'm compelled to draw, right this minute.

"Would you mind if I draw something on your pad?" I ask.

Puck smiles as if he thought I'd never ask. "Yeah, I'd love that," he replies. "You're really talented."

He hands me the pad, helping me position it properly on my lap. Then he pulls a pouch filled with colored pencils from one of the pockets in his cargo shorts. They aren't my preferred medium, but they'll do. Anything that allows me to express myself on paper is phenomenal.

"Will these be okay?" he asks.

"Hell, yeah, they will," I say with a huge smile.

Without thinking, I let my fingers work. I outline, shade, and fill furiously, like a woman possessed. As I draw, I feel better and better. It's good to get whatever this is out of my soul. At first, I don't even know what I'm sketching. I can only see blobs and lines, with no discernable features. Until suddenly, the subject becomes clear. I raise my hands from the paper and assess my creation. It takes my breath away. I've drawn a near perfect representation of the future scene I witnessed with Charmiene. The one where Lottie was gagged and tied up as the seconds to detonation ticked down.

"Whoa," Puck says as he makes out the details.

"Yeah," I say quietly.

It's a lot. I know that. I'm not sure if Puck recognizes Lottie yet, but her features are now clear as day to me.

"Is that…?" he asks.

He sits down hard on a chair beside my bed as he says it. The image seems to be hard for him to process.

"Lottie," we say in unison.

More tears spring to my eyes. I wipe them away quickly. There's no time for crying right now. I remind myself to stay strong and focus. There will be time for all the emotions later. I can even go see a therapist at some point, if I want to and can find a way to afford it. But the most important thing right now is to find Lottie and be sure she's safe.

"Did you hear?" Puck asks reluctantly. "About her… Well… She…"

"I heard that she's missing, if that's what you mean," I say.

He looks immediately relieved that he didn't have to be the one to tell me.

"Good," he breathes. "I mean… Not good that she's missing. Good that you heard. I mean… Not good that you heard because I'm sure that was upsetting. But good that you already know…"

"It's okay," I say, putting the poor guy out of his misery. "I get it. It's a lot for you to take on. I assume Margot and Rags couldn't be here… since you and Grandpa Herbert are alone. Right?"

He nods quickly, his head bobbing so fast it makes me dizzy. "You're right."

"Don't get me wrong," I add. "I'm happy to see you both. Like I said, it means a lot to me that you're here. It's just that I can't help but notice Margot's absence. She was really good to me before my surgery. And my doctor says she made the decision that allowed me to be put on a ventilator. Maybe they would have done that, anyway, if there was no decision maker. But I told them I wanted mine to be Margot just before my surgery, and so she got a chance to step up and make the call when there were complications."

"She's the best," Puck says. "I'm proud that she's my

sister."

"You ought to be," I agree. "She really is the best. She's smart, kind, disciplined, brave. And I trust her completely."

"Me, too," Puck says. "I'd let her make medical decisions for me. Although, I guess Chely would be the one to do that now. She wants to get married, you know? She wants to be my wife."

I'm glad to hear him mention his girlfriend. I know Puck feels a lot of pressure about the baby boy Chely is carrying. The baby is due this summer, and Puck wants to provide for his family and be a good dad. I'm not sure when marriage will come into the picture for him, but I suspect it will at some point soon. He and Chely seem good for each other. But Puck says he's too preoccupied to think about proposing yet.

From what Lottie says and the conversations we've had with Puck, it sounds like he's maturing at warp speed. Working out baggage from childhood will do wonders for a person. Puck sees a psychologist here on the island, Dr. Sally Abbott. It sounds like she's really helping him. By all accounts, Puck is facing his issues with admirable bravery and fortitude. Same as me, though, he has a lot to sort through. Perhaps I should go see Dr. Abbott when I get out of here. I want to continue to heal my emotional wounds, just like Puck.

"How is Chely?" I ask. "Is that baby boy she's growing keeping her on her toes?"

"Oh, he sure is," Puck says. "Chely will be such a good mom... I love her so much. And yeah, she's gotten big lately. She's in the homestretch now, and her belly is huge. Little man kicks her ribs all the time, too."

We chuckle about that. It sounds terribly uncomfortable, but it's the kind of discomfort that's well worth it. Nine months of kicks to the ribs and you're rewarded with a son who will love you for all the days of his life.

The thought stops me cold. Suddenly, I'm overwhelmed with emotion I can't hold back as I think of Mama and how she carried me for nine months, just like Chely is doing for her and Puck's baby boy. I surely kicked Mama's ribs and made her uncomfortable. Then I surely cried and fussed as a baby, then acted out as a curious toddler, and later put her through a number of trials and tribulations as I grew from a child into an adolescent and young adult.

When Mama was growing me in her belly, she probably thought I'd love her for all the days of my life, too. And I do love her. Very much. Yet I haven't spoken to her in years. I left home and ran away, severing our relationship. I'd felt I had no choice. I didn't think she'd accept me as I am. But that's terribly sad. My experience with Charmiene and Pa makes me look at things differently. Not to mention, being seriously injured and almost dying puts things into a new perspective. I need to reach out to Mama. There's no other option. I don't think I can live with myself unless I give Mama every opportunity to have a place in my life. I can be kinder to her. More forgiving. Maybe she can be gentler to me, too.

"Hey, are you okay?" Puck asks, noticing my watery eyes. "Did I say something that upset you?"

We're still getting to know each other. Puck feels uncertain. I don't know for sure what he's thinking either.

We're just going to have to talk through it and continue to learn. We're family. Sort of. I want us to be friends as well.

I shake my head. "No, it wasn't what you said, Puck. I'm glad to hear about Chely and the baby. You three are going to be the best little family. I guess it just made me think of my own mama. I miss her something fierce, especially after what I've just been through. That's all."

He leans forward, interested in what I'm saying. "In Wisconsin?" he asks. "Your mama, I mean. Is she in Wisconsin?"

"Yes," I reply. "I'm from a little town called Fox. It's north of Madison. Beautiful country. My Pa would want me to add that it's Green Bay Packers country."

"Huh," Puck says, and I wonder what he's thinking.

"Why?" I ask.

He hesitates, then jerks his head as if trying to pull himself away from distracting thoughts and back to the present.

"Oh, no reason. Er, I don't know," Puck muses. "I've never been out of Florida. Not even north of Orlando. I guess I wonder what it's like in the rest of the country. And world, for that matter. I see what it looks like on TV, movies, and the internet, but I'd like to see for myself, in person."

"There's plenty of time," I say. "You can go anywhere you want."

He scoffs. "Not exactly. I can't even afford to take care of my family, let alone pay for a trip out of Florida."

His head slumps as he says it, and I feel bad for him.

"Yet," I say.

He looks at me quizzically. "Do you know something I don't?"

Good question on his part. My intuition tells me that Puck will be financially successful in the future. I predict that he'll travel widely with his friends and family. But I don't tell him that. Not all of it. I don't know him well enough to share big predictions like that. It's one thing to read a stranger's palm in Hideaway Park and tell them everything I see. They'll go home and I'll probably never hear from them again. If I'm wrong about what I tell them, they won't hold it against me too hard. But Puck is different. He'll remain in my life. Hopefully, for a long time. I intend to be careful to not get his hopes up. Especially not now. I suspect that my intuition has been affected by my near-death experience. I want to take it for a spin and get a feel for things before I decide how much to count on its accuracy.

"I'm just saying that there's plenty of time left," I clarify. "You're young and healthy. You have your whole life ahead of you. I'm sure there will be time for travel."

"I hope so," he says.

"And hey," I add. "Don't be so hard on yourself about supporting your family. I thought Lottie told me that Grandpa Herbert was going to help you out. Aren't you, Chely, and the baby going to move into his waterfront house?"

Puck sighs heavily. "We are. And I appreciate his generosity. I don't take that lightly. But I still feel badly that I couldn't make a good life for Chely and the baby on my own. I hate that it's only due to inheritance and family money that I'll be able to provide for them. I should have gone to college. And gotten a better job. I should have done a lot of things differently."

"I'm in the same boat there," I say. "I didn't go to

college either. I should have. Maybe I will someday. But don't feel guilty about the family money, Puck. Your grandparents and great-grandparents worked hard and managed their money carefully so they could provide for future generations. Wasn't Herbert's father a coal-industry mogul from up north? I think you should accept the inheritance gratefully. None of us can take the money with us when we go."

"True," he replies. "I hadn't quite thought about it that way. At least, not for long. A thought like that crosses my mind, then I let it slip away, reluctant to believe its truth. I guess the guilt takes over."

I raise my brows to express emphasis. "Then *do* think about it that way. Stop feeling guilty."

Puck laughs. "I'm working on myself. Deep down, I still want to provide Chely and the baby a nice house with blue and white flowers out front, like the yellow one in my early childhood memories. From the time when I still lived with my mom… And I want to do it all on my own."

"Aw," I say. "That's sweet, Puck."

He nods and smiles. "A lot changed for me when I was struck by lightning for the second time, though. It seemed to clear my mind and loosen up a lot that had been hidden away. I feel different. Changed. I don't know how to explain it."

I lean closer to him and put a hand on his forearm. "I know what you mean."

"You do?"

I quickly debate whether I should tell him about my near-death experience. I feel like I can trust him. And I think the two of us understand each other, perhaps more so than any other two people in our group. At least, we do when it comes to matters of life and death and the nature of the Universe. We've been through some unusual shit. There are probably a number of parallels in our experiences.

"I do," I confirm. "I haven't told anyone this yet… Well, I haven't had time…"

"Yeah?" he asks, eyes wide. He's eager for connection with someone who understands him.

"During my surgery, and I guess, after, I had a near-death experience. It's hard to say when because all of time and space sort of swirled together. But, yeah."

"Wow! Really?"

He looks like a kid in a candy store. He's hanging on my every word.

"Really," I confirm. "I left my body and went to this beautiful place. I met a lady who communicated without words. Telepathically, I guess. Then I floated above my body in the operating room. I watched the doctors and nurses working on me. On my body…"

"Were you scared?" he asks.

"Not at all. The sanctuary I was in felt so safe and loving. There was beautiful music. And color. I didn't want to leave."

"Wow," he repeats. "Why did you?"

"Believe it or not, I was given a choice. I could have stayed, if I'd wanted to."

"But you didn't?"

"No. It wasn't my time," I say. "I know that for sure."

We sit in silence, contemplating that statement. It's heavy. I'm glad Puck realizes the weight of the matter. That alone tells me we really do understand each other.

I wonder if he had any otherworldly experiences when he was struck by lightning-- twice. The first time, he was five-years-old and the jolt wiped his memory clean. The second time was a few weeks ago. Puck is thirty-four, and somehow, the repeat strike brought many of his memories back into full view. That's important because the new insight allowed him to figure out what had happened with the mother who abandoned him, and to learn that Lottie and Margot are his sisters. He told us all about it over dinner recently. Being struck twice must put him in the minority of strike victims. It can't possibly happen often. Puck is special.

"I hear that," he confirms. "You're young. You can't be done yet. There's got to be much more for you to do."

"I think so," I reply.

Puck gets quiet again. He's contemplating something serious. His brow furrows and he stares out the window at the beautiful, bright day. It's paradise out there. Like looking at a relaxing screensaver to lower your blood pressure. Only it's beautiful here almost all the time, in real life. Aside from hurricanes, any bad weather we get passes quickly. And when I say quickly, I mean in a matter of hours. It often rains in the afternoon, especially during the summer. The seasonal mid-day rain usually shows up suddenly, comes down hard, then disappears as quickly as it first appeared. I wonder if Puck appreciates the beauty of this island as much as I do. Since he grew up here, I wonder if he takes it for granted.

"What's on your mind?" I ask softly.

"Your drawing," he says, glancing at the sketch of Lottie in my lap. "I know that your intuition is powerful. Do you think…?"

"That this will really happen?"

"Yeah," he replies. "She's my little sister. Even though we just met, I won't let anything happen to Lottie, if I can help it."

"Then we have that in common," I say. "Except…"

"Except you're in here."

"Exactly. But I intend to do everything I can from here. And hopefully, I can heal enough to be discharged soon."

Puck shakes his head hard, then walks over and sits down on the edge of my bed. I get the impression that he's making big decisions in his own heart and mind right. He told me recently that when he has anxious thoughts, he imagines wadding the thoughts up into a tight ball and flinging them away like a basketball. I wonder if he's doing that now.

"Basia, I think we should team up. For real. We're both new to the Callaway family. I mean, Rags is new, too, but you and I are also a lot alike. Seems that way, anyway. I want to help."

"I do, too," I say. "Helping people has always been important to me. And now, it's more important than ever. There are a lot of questions that need answered, though. There are big mysteries to be solved. In a hurry."

"I know."

"You have a baby on the way, Puck. Chely needs you."

He nods. "You're right, but Lottie needs me, too." He stands up and paces in front of the window. "Look, I set out to solve my own mysteries. Before I found out about Margot and Lottie being my sisters, I set out to solve the mystery of who my mom was. I did find out, but she's dead and gone. That mystery didn't have a happy ending. If I can be a part of making sure things turn out better for the rest of my family and friends, I want to do it."

"Wow," I say. "That's really nice of you. It makes sense."

"Then let me help," Puck replies. "I've decided to take some time off from my job at the horse-drawn carriage tour company. Herbert has given me some money that will provide a cushion while I figure things out. He says I'll inherit his money, anyway, so I might as well make use of some of it now, when I need it. The man is very wealthy."

"So, you are very wealthy, too," I add.

"I suppose."

"Own it, Puck. Nothing to be ashamed of," I say.

He shrugs his shoulders. He doesn't want to get into all of that right now. Some topics are still touchy. I get it.

"Whatever, yes," he says. "I hear you. Do we have an agreement?"

Before I can reply, a boom so loud it shakes the hospital sounds from somewhere nearby. Puck rushes to the window and looks out, pressing his face against the glass to see everything in view. He rolls his thumbs and index fingers together as he gazes out. I've never seen him do that before, but he's really pressing hard. It must be a nervous tic.

"What is it?" I ask. "What do you see?"

"I don't know," he says, his voice unsteady. "But a cloud of black smoke is rising in the distance. If I had to guess, I'd say it looks like it's coming from a building down the block. On our side of the street."

16

ROUNDUP

I shift in my bed, determined to get to the window and see for myself what's happening. I grip the side rail with both hands, calculating my path. A week ago, I would have bounded over to the window with the grace and ease of any other young, healthy creature. Now, I move more like a centenarian. A slow one, at that. I can't wait to regain my strength and get my muscles back in shape.

"It's starting," I say out loud, without realizing it.

"What's starting?" Puck asks, turning to face me.

I haven't been out of bed for nearly a week. The cold, hard floor beneath me looks daunting. I'm not sure my legs will hold me if I try to stand. Ishi mentioned that I'd be able to use the bathroom soon, but no doubt, that meant with the help of one of my nurses. I'm not foolish enough to think I can do it on my own yet. At least, not quickly, and not without something sturdy to hold onto. I *just* left the intensive care unit, for Christ's sake. But I really want to get a glimpse of the black smoke. I want to see if it looks like the black smoke from my visions. Maybe I was wrong about Miami. Maybe Hideaway Isle is the target.

"It's a long story," I say. "I'll tell you, but first, can you help me get to the window?"

I'm wearing a blue hospital gown that doesn't close in the back except for one flimsy tie. My hair hasn't been washed. It sits on my head in a matted mess. I probably smell. I'm a little embarrassed but decide this is no time for modesty. And besides, Puck is practically family. He won't care. I reach both of my arms up in the air toward him, much like a baby would do to be picked up out of a crib. I'm determined to get a look at what's happening outside.

"Oh," he says. "You want me to pick you up… and carry you?"

Puck may be dorky, but he's strong. I'm not heavy. Especially after the weight I've lost during my hospital stay. Puck should be able to lift me without any trouble at all.

"Could you?" I plead. "I wouldn't ask. It's just that I've seen an explosion with black smoke, and I want to know if the black smoke you're seeing looks the same."

"To clarify, you've seen this in a vision? Like with your intuition?" he asks.

"Yes, at lunch with Lottie the day I was injured, then during my near-death experience."

"Whoa," Puck says. "Twice, huh?"

"Yeah, I think it was the same scene, anyway. I suppose it could be two separate events. I'm trying to make sense of it. That's why I need to see."

Absentmindedly, I reach a hand down and touch the

sketch pad on my lap. Whatever just boomed outside is connected to my visions. And to Lottie. It has to be. I can feel it. The hairs on the back of my neck stand up and a chill goes down my spine, sealing my certainty.

Puck peers out again, straining to get a full view of the scene as he presses his face against the window.

"It's just out of view from here," he explains. "I think it's on the same side of the street as we are. I can't actually see where the smoke is coming from. I only see the smoke billowing out and around the side. Looks like the breeze is helping blow it into view."

Before I can reply or ask again to be carried to the window, a shrill alarm goes off inside the building. A triangular light mounted above the door to my room lights up in conjunction with the sound. It shines bright white and spins in a tight circle, much like the lights on top of police cars. Overwhelmed by the sensory input, I lift my hands and cover both ears with my palms.

"Damn, that's loud," I mutter.

I'm not sure Puck hears me, but he turns to identify the offending noise and sees the light for himself. He wrinkles his mouth, squinting one eye. His hands remain at his sides. He seems better able to handle the alarm. I guess I'm still touchy, after everything. I feel delicate. And vulnerable. I hate it, but it is what it is.

A woman's voice comes over the loudspeaker.

"Attention, lockdown procedures have been initiated due to an imminent threat to public safety in our area," she says. "You are instructed to shelter in place. Remain where you are. I repeat, shelter in place. Remain where you are until you're told it's safe to move. More information will be announced as we receive it. I repeat, shelter in place."

My eyes widen as Puck and I look at each other, unsure of what to do. I admit, I'm scared. I'm in no position to take basic care of myself, let alone protect myself from an imminent threat. What do they even mean by that?

"Puck," I say. "I'm afraid. I'm sorry to say that. I wish I wasn't, but I'm scared to death. What do we do?"

He takes a breath and, within a few short moments, it's like something kicks into gear.

"Sit tight," he says. "I'll keep you safe. But first, I need to find out where everyone else is. Starting with Herbert."

He yanks his phone out of his pocket and dials. Thankfully, he still has a signal. He waits eagerly while it rings.

"Pop!" he yells when Herbert picks up.

Puck doesn't bother to explain that he grew up thinking of Herbert as his adoptive father. It wasn't until a few weeks ago that he learned Herbert is actually his grandpa. No explanation is needed, anyway. Puck had already told us a lot about his discovery, then Margot filled us in on details we'd missed. I think Puck is still deciding what he'll call Herbert long term. He might stick with Pop.

"Thank God," I mumble.

"Where are you? Are you okay?"

He puts the phone on speaker so I can hear the conversation, too.

"Fine," Herbert says.

I immediately notice that there's no alarm sounding in the background on the other end of the line.

"Grandpa Herbert?" I ask. "I'm here also. It's Basia."

I didn't have to tell him my name. I'm a little nervous, and it shows. Oh, well. I tell myself being nervous right now is understandable.

"Basia, dear," Herbert replies. "Good to hear your voice. I'm safe and sound. No need to worry about me. I see the smoke in the distance, but I'm a ways off from it. Maybe a gas leak or something. I hope no one was hurt."

Puck visibly relaxes. "Where, exactly, are you?" he asks.

"I walked down by the art museum. Thought I'd find something to pass the time. It seemed like the two of you had a lot to talk about. I was just about to go inside."

I remember Puck telling us that the art museum was one of Herbert and his wife's favorite places to go together. I know he must miss her something fierce. I've never been to the museum, myself. I'd like to go, especially since I'm an artist. Maybe Herbert can show me around the museum someday soon.

"Good," Puck says. "That's the opposite direction from the smoke."

"I know," Herbert replies. "Should I head back to the hospital? Do you need me to drive you home, Puck?"

"No!" Puck and I exclaim together, our voices rising.

"We're under lockdown here," Puck explains. "Can you hear the alarms in the background?"

"Lockdown?" Herbert asks, his voice breaking ever so slightly.

I think my heart breaks a little along with it. He's worried about us. The feeling is mutual. Thoughts of what happened to Lottie and Margot's Grandpa Vern come to mind. I don't like the idea of Herbert being out there by himself without Puck to watch over him. From what I understand, Herbert has been out of sorts since his wife, Mildred, died. That was less than a month ago. They'd been married for decades. Something like sixty years if I'm remembering correctly. I imagine the man feels lost and alone. Frankly, I'm impressed that he's putting on such a brave face. I think I'd be a sobbing, miserable mess if I'd just lost Lottie after sixty years of marriage. Not Herbert. He's out doing things like visiting me in the hospital and making me feel like part of a family that my girlfriend only just recently found out she had.

The last thing I want to see happen is for Herbert to get tangled up in a dangerous situation like Grandpa Vern did. Lottie would never forgive herself. And besides, Herbert is the eldest member of Lottie's family on both sides. His perspective and grandfatherly guidance is invaluable. He's a treasure. Not to mention, when Puck and Chely's baby boy is born, Herbert will become a great-grandfather. We most certainly want to keep the man alive and well for as long as we possibly can.

"I'm sure it's a routine precaution," Puck says.

He's taking on a number of new roles lately. One of those is that of a leader who others look up to for guidance. Puck knows his world is changing. So far, it seems like he's taking it in stride. I admire him for that. Both Puck and Herbert are good men. I'm grateful to have them in my life.

"Do you really think so?" Herbert asks. "Or are you trying to make an old man feel better about his loved ones being stuck inside while danger lurks nearby?"

Puck shudders. His reaction is so visceral that it's obvious to me something has rattled him.

"What is it?" I ask, hopefully quiet enough that Herbert doesn't hear.

Puck presses the mute button.

"Nothing," he says. "It was just the way he described danger lurking nearby. It reminded me of all the bad dreams I've had about sharks. Have you heard about me and my silly fear of sharks? Most of my life, I've wanted to gather up all the shark teeth from the sea around our little island so that I could finally rest. I used to go to the beach to hunt for them every single morning. I know it's bizarre, but..."

My eyes light up. Not because I want Puck to be scared, but because his shark dreams sound an awful lot like my wolf dreams. I like the fact that we're finding so many similarities between us. I think we truly can be good friends.

"I haven't heard," I say. "But I used to have terrible dreams about a wolf named Echo. I might know a little something about how you feel."

"Puck?" Herbert says, interrupting our bonding. "Did you put me on hold, son? Are you telling Basia about your shark dreams and the collection of teeth you store under your bed?"

"Under your bed?" I ask. "That's hard core."

He shrugs and we chuckle together. Herbert knows Puck so well. Puck unmutes the phone, bringing Herbert back into the conversation.

"I am," he confirms. "It was something about the way you said it."

"I know," Herbert says. "I heard it as it came out of my mouth. I'm pretty sure it was the word lurking."

"Probably so," Puck replies. "But I'm trying hard to put all of that behind me. The more I face my problems in real life, the less I find myself scared of sharks and their horrible teeth."

I nod emphatically. He's got that right. I make a mental note to circle back to this topic sometime soon. Puck and I probably have plenty of notes to compare. Maybe my experience standing up to Echo could help him face his fear of sharks. Maybe we can help each other. I know how menacing big teeth can be, too. I may have stood up to Echo, but remembering his threatening presence sends a shiver down my spine.

"At any rate," Herbert continues, "I don't want to leave the two of you alone during the lockdown. I think I should head back and join you."

"Dad…" Puck says before correcting himself. "Grandpa, I don't think they're letting anyone in either. The announcement said to shelter in place. I don't want you anywhere near all of this. In fact, I'm going to have someone pick you up and take you home where it's safe."

"Nonsense," Herbert says. "I'm the one who should be looking out for you, Puck. You're my boy. I can't let anything happen to you."

Tears well up in Puck's eyes. I can practically see the wheels turning in his mind as he tries to figure out what to do.

"Dad, I'm sorry, but I won't have it. I don't mean any disrespect, but I don't want you in harm's way. You let me take care of myself and Basia. We're okay here."

"Puck…"

"I'm calling someone to come get you. Are you in front of the art gallery?"

"Yes, by the ticket booth," Herbert confirms, submitting to Puck's insistence.

"Stay put. I'm going to ask Chevelle. She'll be in Knick Knack. That's what she calls her little red car."

"Well… okay," Herbert confirms.

Puck's fingers move like the wind as he texts Chevelle. She responds immediately, agreeing to get Herbert and be sure he's safe. Puck breathes a huge sigh of relief once that's settled.

I watch and listen as he places a call to Chely. She picks up and chats for a few minutes. She'd been at their loft on the other side of the island and hadn't seen or heard the boom. She had no idea that anything unusual was going on until Puck called. He tells her to stay at home and to lock the doors until she hears from him again. Satisfied that she's safe, Puck disconnects the call.

He throws his head back and closes his eyes tightly for a moment.

"Everything okay?" I ask.

He shakes his head to clear the anxiety. "Yeah," he replies, opening his eyes again. "A lot of people are counting on me. I'm still trying to figure out how to be my best for them."

"I know," I say. "You're doing it."

He picks his phone up again and stares at it.

"You thinking about calling Margot?" I ask.

"I am, but I don't think she'll be able to answer. I already tried to call her on my way here, when I got news that you were awake and being moved to a regular room. I think Margot and Rags may have turned their phones off while they look for Lottie. I'm not sure where they are or what they're doing. They told me they'd get in touch as soon as they could."

I nod. I want to ask more about what Margot and Rags said before they left to look for Lottie, but this isn't really the time. The alarm still blares in the background and the light still flashes. I'm compelled to focus on the present. If this injury and hospital stay has taught me anything, it's to keep my attention fixed on what I can do rather than to get bogged down in all the things I can't control. That lesson is sinking in deep, taking hold of me at the most fundamental level. It's a good thing.

"Okay," I reply. "I don't mean to be a pain, but I'd really like to get to that window. Can you still see the smoke?"

Puck glances out again. "Yeah. There's more of it, and it's even blacker than before. Hold on. I'll help you get over here to see for yourself."

17

THE FEW

Puck has me in his arms and on the way to the window when we hear the metal latch on the door open. I'm so focused on the window that I don't bother to turn back and look at who it is. Puck does, though, and he hastily sets me down in a chair.

"Can we help you?" he asks the visitor.

Using all my strength, I pull my face to the window. Finally, I can see what Puck has seen. The smoke is pouring out from a building down the block. It's black, alright, just like the smoke in my visions. From what I understand, the darker the smoke, the hotter and more volatile the fire. I tremble thinking about Lottie tied up as the bomb counted down. We aren't in Miami, and I really feel like what I saw was in Miami. I hope I'm not wrong about that, though.

Generally, my intuition arrives and then it's the job of my mind to interpret it. Sometimes, I mess it up. Signals get crossed. Or I assume too much. It isn't an exact science, that's for sure. If only I could find a way to fine tune my abilities. If I'm going to find Lottie-- or help Nigel and his friend, or anyone else, for that matter-- I must find a way.

I sense Puck's apprehension about the visitor, so I glance to see who it is. I don't recognize the man, but he doesn't strike me as a threat.

"Basia Guthrie?"

"Who's asking?" Puck replies.

"Tom Marsh," he says, reaching out to shake Puck's hand. "Hideaway Isle Police Department. I'm the lead investigator on Basia's case."

Puck doesn't shake Tom's hand. He's skeptical.

"How did you get in here?" Puck asks. "I thought the hospital was on lockdown."

Tom steps back, respectful of Puck's protectiveness.

"I was already inside the building when they initiated lockdown. I thought the staff had told Basia I was coming."

"They did," I say.

"Good," Tom replies, turning to me with a kind smile. "Ms. Guthrie, do you mind if I ask you a few questions?"

Puck puts a hand up to stop me. "Do you have identification on you?" he asks Tom. "A badge?"

Tom smiles again. "Of course."

He opens his jacket to reveal a badge next to a holstered weapon on his belt, then he slowly reaches into his pocket and retrieves his black leather wallet. He flips the wallet open and holds his Hideaway Isle P.D. identification card out where we can read it.

Puck relaxes. I can't begin to express how much I appreciate him looking out for me like this. He's going to make such a good dad.

"Sorry," Puck says. "Can't be too careful… these days, and under, well, these circumstances."

"Understood," Tom says. "You're Puck Reed, right? Margot and Lottie Callaway's older brother?"

"I am," Puck replies, then corrects himself. "I mean, we don't have DNA tests or anything, but we compared pictures of our mom. It's the same woman. Annie Reed, who later became Annie Callaway."

Tom nods like he already knows the whole story. When he does, something about the look on his face clicks and I remember him from the investigation a few weeks ago, after Llew Brackus held us hostage. I can't believe I didn't recognize him right away. He interviewed me down at the station. I wonder if I'm losing it. I wouldn't be surprised if my mental capacities have taken a hit after what I've been through. Hopefully, any deficiencies will be short term. I intend to get back to full capacity. And if I'm lucky, I'll get even better as I develop my intuition and intellect.

"I remember you!" I say, and Puck looks even more relieved when I do.

Tom smiles. "I'm not sure if Margot or Lottie told you, but I'm an old friend of their dad's," he explains. "Jon Callaway and I went to school together, back in the old days when this island wasn't crawling with tourists." He chuckles about that last part, as if he's letting us in on a little-known secret.

He smells like cigarettes and coffee, just the same as he did before. I should have recognized him from the potent smell alone. It fills the room. The lines on Tom's face show more wear and tear than I suspect most men his age have accumulated, but his eyes are friendly. I get the idea that he is a good man. I feel safer knowing he's in here with us, at least, until this lockdown is over and we know what caused the black smoke down the block.

"Margot told me," I say.

Puck obviously didn't know because he looks a little confused.

"We grew up together. Jon was a fine man. I know he'd want me to take good care of his daughters, and that extends to the two of you as well," Tom explains.

Something about the way he says it piques my curiosity. I believe him. It isn't that I don't. Maybe being happy that Tom is in here with us was shortsighted. Maybe there's an important reason that he's in here and not out there investigating. Maybe he thinks we're somehow connected to whatever is happening out there. And maybe that's bad news. Far worse news than I'd expected when Dr. Khatri told me Tom wanted to speak with me. I had assumed that was all about Nigel and my injury.

"Thank you," I say. "I've been going over what I think are relevant details in my mind. It's given me something to pass the time while waiting on my body to heal. I hope I can help connect some dots for you. I'm anxious to get this investigation going."

Tom gestures to a chair near me, asking if he can sit. I nod to say that he can, and Puck takes a seat on the side of the hospital bed nearby.

"That's good of you," Tom says. "I hear you're a psychic, too. Do I have that right?"

I blush. I don't like people knowing about that. I especially don't like them talking about it. I'm not seeking fame or notoriety. I just want to live a peaceful life. I swear. Tom notices my apprehension and slows down.

"I'm sorry," he says. "That was too forward. Please forgive me. I just meant to say that I'm happy to have your input. I think you could potentially be a wonderful asset in your own case. Maybe even beyond."

"Beyond?" I ask, whipping my head around to meet Tom's gaze.

I hadn't thought about anything beyond my circle of family and friends. At least, not much beyond them. I'd want to help thwart the big Miami attack I saw if it will really come to pass, and if I possibly could. Maybe that's the kind of thing Tom is talking about. But what does he think I can do? And what does he know that he isn't telling us?

"Maybe," Tom replies.

Puck shifts uncomfortably on the bed. He's fidgety and doesn't seem to know what to do with his hands. He folds them awkwardly on his lap, but it looks forced. All this family leadership is new to him. It's the first time he's had a family to protect, much less practice doing so.

My attention is pulled to the scene outside again, and I can't help but notice the parallel to the picture windows in my near-death experience with Charmiene. Not to mention, the black smoke against the vivid blue sky and sparkling waters around our island seems like an especially onerous contrast. There shouldn't be smoke like this in paradise.

"What are you seeing out there?" Tom asks.

He stands and walks to the window to follow my gaze. When he sees the smoke, he purses his lips, then sits back down in his chair.

"Something's burning," I say.

"Yes, you're right about that," he adds. "I didn't know you'd be able to see it from here."

"It sounds like you already know what's going on," Puck says. "Care to share?"

"Yeah," I add. "And why are you in here instead of out solving that case?"

I point towards the window for emphasis, then smooth my blonde hair down over my shoulders, suddenly self-conscious about the way I look. I don't know why. I'm sure Tom has seen worse. I'm beginning to get very tired. It's been quite a while that I've been awake and moving around now. My body isn't used to it. I tell myself to stay alert and hold on. I'm not sure how I'd sleep with the alarm blaring, anyway. The alarm will, apparently, continue to sound as long as lockdown is in effect.

Tom takes a deep breath before answering. I suspect he's already talked to Dr. Khatri about my condition. He had probably been advised to go easy on me. I turn to look outside again. It's hard to look away. I just want to *see* the smoke. To compare it to my vision. I can't quite tell if it's the same as what I saw. The smoke is certainly the same color, but the settling looks different. I wonder if it's due to my vantage point. Charmiene seemed to shift things around when I needed her to so I could see from different angles. I wish I could somehow do that now.

Tom suddenly sits up straight. An idea has come to him.

"Say, Basia," he begins, raising a finger to his chin as he thinks.

"Yeah?"

"I couldn't help but notice the sketch on your bed. Did you draw it?" he asks.

His eyes are wide with interest, although I'm not sure what he's getting at.

"Yes, I did."

"Nice work," he adds. "You draw portraits for tourists in Hideaway Park, don't you?"

"I do."

"I hear you're very good at it. And you read their palms?"

"Yes," I say, wondering what he's angling for. "Why?"

He smiles, his finger still on his chin. "I don't know. Maybe this is a longshot, but have you ever thought about combining those two abilities-- your psychic powers and your art?"

I cock my head to one side. It's an interesting thought. Without waiting for me to respond, Tom practically leaps out of his seat and rushes to the sketch of Lottie.

"She just drew that, less than an hour ago," Puck adds. He seems intrigued by Tom's idea. "Are you saying she could draw what she sees in her mind's eye, and that the drawings might help solve mysteries?"

Puck is articulating what's swirling around in my mind. They just might be onto something here.

"Maybe!" I say enthusiastically.

"May I?" Tom asks.

I nod, giving him permission to pick up my sketch. He does so, gleefully. He seems to get quite a kick out of solving things. I suppose that's an asset in his job. He probably does puzzles in his spare time, for fun. I'll bet he'd go crazy for murder mystery dinner theater and escape games.

Puck stands, partially to get out of Tom's way as he examines my drawing, but also because he's getting excited, too.

"That's Lottie," Puck offers. "I can recognize her, plain as day. Basia is really worried about her."

Tom nods quickly. "I see it, too. The representation is remarkable. Such talent."

As Tom says this, I can't help but wonder why he hasn't mentioned Nigel or my injury. Nigel doesn't seem to be at the top of his list of priorities. That worries me. There must be bigger concerns to tend to.

"I am worried about Lottie," I add. "I've been told that she's gone. That she disappeared. No one seems to know where she is. I hear that Margot and Rags are out looking for her. Are the police looking for her, too?"

Tom takes another deep inhale, then seems to hold his breath. "Sort of."

That answer enrages me. I'm a person who stays pretty even keel, but I feel anger rise to my face with a warm rush. At least Margot and Rags are doing something. They're not sitting back and saying things like sort of. Do the police around here take no responsibility? What in the hell?

"Excuse me, but what?" I reply.

Puck lowers his brow. He seems to want to be on Tom's side, to cheer the man on to victory. But he's unsure. I don't blame him.

"Stay with me for a minute," Tom says. "This sketch. Did you decide what you were going to draw before you put pencil to paper?"

I shake my head. "No, I felt compelled to draw. Puck said he had a sketchpad, so I used it. I let my fingers do the work and the image seemed to fly out of me."

Tom grins. "That's what I hoped you'd say. Can we try something?"

I'm somewhat reluctant. I don't like the feeling of being a lab rat. But my hands do want to draw again. They feel heavy, like they're weighed down by an image that wants to come forth into the light of day. I assume Tom wants me to draw something, so I decide to cooperate. It will be good for my mind and spirit.

"Okay, sure," I reply.

"Great!" Tom exclaims, turning to a new, blank page on the sketchpad and handing me a colored pencil. "Here, I want you to disconnect your thinking mind. Let it go limp and blank. Draw what I need to know about the smoke down the street. Let the image come through you. Do you understand what I'm saying?"

I look at him curiously. I've never had anyone in a position of authority believe in me like this. Mrs. McClanahan thought I had a knack for history back in high school, but this is on a whole other level. Tom is looking to my psychic abilities to help with his investigation. It reminds me of the old TV show called *Medium* starring Patricia Arquette. It was supposedly based on a real woman who helped a police department solve cases. Aunt Portia showed it to me when she was helping me hone my abilities. I wonder if I could be of help to our local police department. I'd love that. I could be the drawing medium, or something. I'd come up with a better name than that. Is that what Tom is thinking?

"Okay," I say, taking the sketchpad and pencil from Tom's eager hands. "I'll do my best."

"That's all I ask," Tom says.

He and Puck look at each other expectantly, like they've just discovered something big. They even high five each other. Such a guy thing to do. I chuckle as I get into the zone. The alarm in the background makes it hard, but it isn't much different than a crowd of tourists talking and laughing in the park when you get right down to it. I close my eyes, smoothing the surface of the cool paper with my palm. It only takes a few seconds until my hands are frantic, moving over the paper with the pencil at high speed.

I let my fingers carry me, just like I did when I sketched the image of Lottie. Large strokes, small strokes, and dots become joined as one cohesive piece. I shade, then swirl, circling around the paper like mad. As I draw, I tell myself to be a vessel. To let whatever the source of my intuition is take over and sweep me up. I thank the powers that be for the gifts I've been given, and I ask that my gifts might be used for good. I don't stop sketching until I'm certain I'm done. By the time I look up, Tom's mouth is hanging wide open as he stares at my work.

"What is it?" I ask.

Then I follow his gaze and see for myself. It isn't obvious until I hold the sketch out a little and take it in from a bit of a distance. It's Llew Brackus, plain as day. I've drawn him standing in front of the burning building. There's so much detail in the building and in his face that there can be no mistaking.

"Wow," I say quietly.

I'm reminded that we never heard what happened to Llew after the day he held us hostage. Margot shot him in the gut while rescuing Lottie. Llew was in bad shape, bleeding out the last time we saw him. He was taken away by ambulance, but we weren't told whether he lived or died. At least, I wasn't told. Maybe Margot and Rags know by now. Tom promised Llew would be prosecuted to the fullest extent of the law. Could Llew be out there orchestrating bombings? He was after Lottie's money before. Llew said Lottie owed him due to Annie's debt that went unpaid when she died. There are a million things I'd like to know, beginning with whether Llew is still alive.

"Who is that?" Puck asks. "He kind of looks like me."

"Huh," I say.

I hadn't thought about it before, but Llew does look a little like Puck. That's weird. Llew is pure evil, though. The complete opposite of Puck. Llew's villainous expression and Puck's friendly, good-natured one take away from the similarities in their features.

Tom snaps a picture of my sketch with his phone, then stands and rushes toward the door. He doesn't stop to answer Puck's question.

"Thank you, Basia!" Tom exclaims. "I'll be back soon. But right now, I have to go."

The door slams hard behind him, and I'm left in shock and awe at what just happened. I fill Puck in on what I know about Llew, then we marvel together at my drawing. Maybe I'm onto something.

18

HOLDING

Funny enough, the rest of the day is uneventful. It has to be. At least, it does in my little world. I'm far too exhausted to do anything but conk out shortly after Tom leaves.

Puck helps me to the bathroom. Then I fall asleep in my hospital bed, even as the alarm continues to blare. I'm not sure how long lockdown remains in effect. I think I notice Agnes coming in to check on me throughout the night, but I sleep so hard that I'm not sure whether she's real or a dream. My body needs rest to heal. No way around it. And as exhilarating as the process of sketching for Tom turned out to be, it took a toll on my energy reserves.

When I awaken, it's early in the morning. I can tell by the angle of the sun coming through the window and the dimness of the light outside. It's golden hour. The sun is making its way up and into the sky. I'm not usually awake this early, but I rather like the mood. Maybe I'll make a point to get up and watch the sun rise once I'm back in my RV and life is back to normal. Maybe I'll make Lottie wake up with me so we can watch it together.

I can hardly wait until she's found. Maybe today will be the day. She *has* to be okay. She just has to be.

I'm not sure what time I fell asleep, but the sun hadn't set when I closed my eyes. I'm not sure I even made it to mid-afternoon yesterday. Oh, well. If I slept that hard for that long, my body must have needed it. I know I must pace myself and listen to my body. Pushing it will only hurt me, and then I won't be able to help anyone.

I raise my head and look around. My room appears the same as I remember it. The alarms have stopped. That must be good news. Whatever the crisis was, it's apparently over now. At first, I think I'm alone. Then my sleepy eyes land on Puck. He's got both of the chairs in the room pushed together, his long limbs piled on top. He looks uncomfortable, but he's sound asleep. My heart warms as I take it in. Puck has a very pregnant girlfriend and an elderly grandfather to look after, yet he's here with me. Not to mention, he's skipped his morning ritual of picking up shark teeth on the beach in favor of being here. That speaks volumes. It also indicates that Puck is progressing in his own life. He's growing up. And showing up.

I'm not sure what I did to deserve a friend like Puck, but I'll take it. He's such a good guy. It means so much that he is sticking with me like this. I'm not sure how I'll ever be able to repay him for his kindness, but I'll certainly try. I intend to be the best friend I can possibly be.

Careful to stay extra quiet so as not to wake him, I reach for the call button. Whether I like it or not, I need a nurse to help me get to the bathroom. I push the button, and a few minutes later, Agnes walks in, all smiles. She looks like a proud parent whose child has just graduated from something. I suppose I have graduated from something. And Agnes should be proud. She played an important part in my healing. It takes a village.

I smile back. "Shh," I say. "My friend is asleep."

Aren't I great at stating the obvious?

"I see," Agnes says, moving quickly to my side. "Are you ready to use the potty?"

I laugh, as quietly as I can. I find the word potty funny, as well as the way Agnes jumped right in without so much as saying hello. It feels like it's been a long time since the day of my surgery when I saw her last. I've been through so much since then. I raise a hand over my mouth to hold my laughter in. Once I've regained my composure, I whisper my response.

"And hello to you, too," I reply. "Nice to see you after my surgery, intensive care stay, and near-death experience."

I'm not sure why I'm feeling sarcastic, but I am. I don't think Agnes minds. It's all in good fun. I'm in a jovial mood this morning. I'm no expert in psychology, but I think I'm feeling better because I was useful yesterday. Doing that sketch for Tom seemed to actually help. I'm excited about the prospect of drawing more. I like thinking of myself as the drawing medium, although still I intend to come up with a catchier title. Drawing like I did yesterday just might be the perfect method to harness my psychic powers in a way that can be put to good use.

"Girl," Agnes says, "I've been checking on you all night. I've seen plenty of you."

We chuckle together. I really like Agnes. I wish she and I could be friends in real life, outside of this hospital. She's old enough to be my mother, but I don't think that would stop us. I can imagine getting together for coffee or lunch. Agnes might even like Jimmy Buffet. We could head over to Key West one day and have a meal at Margaritaville. Lottie could come, too.

"Fine," I say. "Yes, I'm ready for the bathroom. Past ready."

"Well, let's get you there, then," she says. "We'll talk about that near-death experience once you've had a chance to empty your bladder."

She opens a closet door in one corner of the room that I hadn't even noticed, then pulls out a walker. For some reason, it catches me off guard. I would have expected a wheelchair, maybe, but a walker seems like we're skipping a step-- or two. I'm not sure I'll be able to stand for any length of time, even with the support of a walker. It seems so cold and exposed.

"Oh, I don't know..." I say.

Agnes shakes her head. "I do. Come on, swing your legs around the side of the bed and I'll help you stand."

"Are you a drill sergeant in another life?" I joke. "Is this nurse gig just something you do on the side?"

I'm enjoying the rapport we have going on, but I don't see myself able to get around with just a walker. Not yet. I want Agnes to hold me up. I know she can't carry me like Puck did last night. She can surely help support my weight, though.

"Trust me," she says, her deep brown eyes full of

wisdom. "The sooner you get moving, the better you'll heal. I know you don't want to be stuck in here with me any longer than you have to."

I shrug. "You're not so bad." We smile. "But I do want to get out of here and help find my girlfriend. She's missing."

I swing my legs over the side of the bed, like Agnes asked. My feet dangle, hovering just above the surface of the cool linoleum floor. I kick one foot absentmindedly, deciding whether I can really get to the bathroom using this contraption. It seems so flimsy compared to my weakness. It seems like I need my weight supported more surely. I assume my head is delicate. I fear banging it on something if I should fall. The last thing I want is to backslide and have to spend more time here. God forbid I have another brain bleed and need another surgery. That is not going to happen. It can't. I might not be able to bear it.

"Ah, Lottie, yes?" Agnes asks.

"How do you know her name?"

"You said it enough times the day of your surgery. Seemed like every other breath, you were asking for her… asking where she was. It was a sad, sad thing to watch. I went home that night and told my husband how sad it was."

Agnes gives me a half-smile that exposes one big dimple. I hardly know this woman, but I feel like I love her. Is that strange? Maybe I've gotten overly sentimental due to everything that's happened to me. Like I said, I feel different since waking up from the near-death experience. My perspective on life is… more mature, for lack of a better description. Where I was once in the ocean being knocked about by every metaphorical wave that passed my way, I'm now on a pier above the water, watching the waves break below. The distance changes things.

"That's nice of you," I reply. "To care so much."

Agnes winks at me, her dimple still on display. "Part of the job." She glances at Puck, who is still sleeping like a baby. He must have been even more exhausted than I was. "Did you find her?"

"Lottie?"

"Duh," she says playfully. "Who else?"

I shake my head. "No, I didn't. We didn't. At least, no one is telling me."

"Why do you say it like that?" Agnes asks. "Do you think your family and friends would lie to you?"

She glances at Puck.

"He's Lottie and Margot's big brother," I say. "We've become friends."

"I wasn't necessarily talking about him," she clarifies. "Or maybe I was. Answer the question."

I'm kind of surprised by how forward Agnes is being. I wonder if she knows something specific that she's trying to tell me. If she does, I wish she'd come right out with it. After I get to the bathroom, that is. The pressure in my bladder is killing me. As much as I want to hear what she has to say, I want more to make it to the toilet without having an accident.

"No, I don't think they'd lie to me," I say. "But I've got to pee, Agnes. Please, help me get to the bathroom, or bring me a bedpan. I can't wait much longer."

"That's from the fluids we've been giving you in your IV line," she says. "It's good. Your body is working correctly, doing what it should."

I nod, then reach for the damned walker Agnes has positioned in front of me.

"Will this thing slip and knock me on my ass?"

Agnes laughs. "Probably not."

Only partially satisfied with that answer, I press on, gripping the handlebars and pulling with all my might until I'm off the bed. Agnes puts a firm hand on my back as I gather the momentum to inch forward.

"You've got it," she says. "You're doing it."

I have to concentrate hard, so I just nod. I don't have the wherewithal to talk during what feels like a Herculean effort to shuffle my feet while maintaining my balance. Funny how something so simple can become suddenly foreign and difficult. In a way, it feels like I'm learning to walk all over again. And I was only out of commission for less than a week. I can hardly fathom what happens to people in comas for longer. Or those that have broken legs, or necks, or backs.

When I'm better, I want to volunteer at the hospital. I might even want to work here someday. Maybe I'll find a way to go back to school and study to become a medical professional. I'd never considered such a thing before, but it now seems like the perfect choice for me. I can see it now-- I spend part of my time working at the hospital to save people or help them recover from injuries like mine. The other part of my time will be spent as the drawing medium, helping police to solve cases and catch criminals. Although maybe that's too much for one person. Maybe I'm getting ahead of myself. I'm just so excited to be able to help. I've always liked to help, and especially now, I understand more about the kind of help that's needed. There's so much to do. So many roles to fill. I'll bet hospital jobs come with great health insurance.

Health insurance. Oops. I hadn't thought of it since before my surgery. How had it slipped my mind since? I hate the way my thinking has become so scattered lately. I can only focus on matters of limited scope at once. I hope that will get better as I heal. I don't want to be scatterbrained. It's embarrassing. At the same time, though, I can't be too upset with myself. What I've been through is a lot. I think I should cut myself some slack.

"What's on your mind?" Agnes asks as she helps me lower myself onto the toilet and pee. "I see you studying about something. Care to share?"

"You want to talk while I pee?" I ask.

The relief of emptying my bladder is tremendous. My whole body wriggles with pleasure as the urine comes out. So, this is what's become of me.

"You have something better to do?" she asks with a smile.

I wipe, then stand to wash my hands. Every movement takes effort, but I'm getting the hang of this. Maybe the walker isn't so bad.

"I guess not," I reply as I towel my hands off and wipe my face, careful not to be too rough on my head. "I was just thinking about the bills that will come from this stay. I don't have insurance."

Agnes shrugs. "I see."

She helps me back to the bed, although I mostly do it myself. Agnes was right. I am more capable than I realized. I'm glad she pushed me. Once I'm back in bed with the covers tucked in at my sides, she sits down beside me. She glances at Puck. He's still sleeping soundly. He must not be a morning person.

"The question I asked you…"

"Yeah?"

"Allow me to rephrase it," she says.

"Okay," I say. I'm not sure what she's getting at.

"Do you think your friends and family would keep things from you? Not lie outright, mind you, but withhold information?"

She stares directly into my eyes as she waits for an answer. I consider her question carefully before I answer.

"Maybe," I say. "If they thought it was in my best interest. They're good people."

Agnes sighs, then smooths the blanket around the side of the mattress, tracing it with her strong, yet delicate fingertips. Those hands have surely seen so many blankets. So many fabrics have, no doubt, been smoothed as serious matters were pondered.

"Basia, I notice you don't have a phone or computer in here. And the TV hasn't been on."

"That's true," I say. "You told me not to watch TV or look at the internet on the day of my surgery. Remember?"

"This isn't that day," Agnes says, measuring her words.

It might be my imagination, but I think I notice one of her eyelids twitch at the corner. It's almost imperceptible.

"True."

She stands, a decision made.

"I have to step out for a few minutes," she says, winking and taking her phone out of her pocket. She sets it down on the side table next to my bed. "I seem to have lost my smartphone. I'm sure it will turn up soon."

I nod my understanding.

"I never lock it," she adds. "Anyone could pick it up and use it. They could connect to the internet, make calls… Whatever they wanted. But oh, well. I'm sure it will turn up soon."

With another wink, she scoots out the door, and I pick up her phone.

19

THE NERVE

I've felt contemplative for the past week that I've been in the hospital. I'm naturally that way, despite what the tourists in Hideaway Park would probably report. I'm an introvert, believe it or not. I don't have social anxiety or anything like that, and I enjoy being around other people. But I need my downtime to recharge, too. I'm an observer who likes to ponder the depth of things. It isn't enough for me to scratch the surface. I want to know the down and dirty, nitty gritty details of why people are the way they are. I want to know what makes them tick. I want to know them well so I can choose carefully.

I actually think Margot and I might have that in common. I'm sure it comes from having to rely so heavily on myself most of my life. If I'm going to trust someone, I want to be absolutely positive that trust is deserved. I need to know that I'm not going to be disappointed. I get the idea Margot feels the same way. She's more sensitive than Lottie. She takes things more personally. Margot and I have never talked about it, but I think I understand why.

Puck is a lot like us, too. It feels good to have found people who understand my temperament and what makes me tick.

As I consider what my friends and family may or may not be withholding from me, I attempt to put myself in their shoes. I ask myself what I would do if the tables were turned and someone I loved was injured and hospitalized with a brain bleed that required surgery and a stint in intensive care. I understand the strong desire to protect me. And I appreciate it. Truly, I do. They must think that I'll backslide if I get too upset. Maybe they're right. I've never been injured like this before, and I honestly don't know how important it is to remain calm as I get better. I know the brain is delicate. But I want to be told the truth. In my view, ignorance is not bliss.

Glancing at Puck once more, I decide it's now or never. He's still out cold. I take a cleansing breath and open Agnes' phone.

"Here goes nothing," I mumble out loud.

Like Agnes promised, the phone is unlocked and I can do anything I want with it. I smile when I see her background photo. It's her with what appear to be her husband and adult children. They're sprawled out on the steps of a tropical swimming pool, palm trees in the background and drinks in hand, their brown skin practically glowing in the sun. They all look happy. I'm glad to see their faces. If Agnes and I become friends, I'll get to meet these happy people. I look forward to that someday.

Getting down to business, I begin by navigating to the internet and checking local news. Most of our news comes out of Miami, but there's a little paper published in Key West called the *Key West Citizen* that reports Hideaway Isle stories as well. I know the website URL, so I type it in, then scan the featured stories. I didn't find anything interesting in the Miami Herald paper that Hebert had yesterday. I hope I have better luck this time, although I don't know what I'm looking for. I suppose I'll know it when I see it.

It doesn't take long. The very first story is about yesterday's explosion. I click on it and hold my breath as I wait for the full article to load. Visions of the big Miami explosion that Charmiene showed me come flooding back. I want to understand. I want to know what I can do to prevent the big one from happening. As the article loads and I read, I'm shocked. It mentions not just one explosion, but a series of them having rocked the Keys over the past week. It says there have been five explosions in total-- one in each of Key Largo, Key West, Islamorada, Marathon, and our very own Hideaway Isle.

No one knows who is behind the blasts, but each time the location has been an abandoned building near a populated area. So far, no one has been injured. Authorities aren't sure what the motive is. Apparently, a psychologist out of Massachusetts has been called in to help with profiling in an effort to catch the bomber before anyone is hurt. The article is brief. It sticks to the facts and doesn't spend time with speculation or conjecture. I'm sure the TV news will do plenty of that.

I shake my head. This is an interesting development. The fact that I sketched Llew outside the burning building down the block is especially puzzling. What would he have to do with these explosions? Even if he is behind them by some chance, what is the goal of blowing up abandoned buildings? My blood runs cold as I answer my own questions. What if these explosions are a trial run for the big one? I shudder at the thought. It's terrifying.

"Whatcha doing?" Puck asks sleepily from his spot on the chair.

I jerk, caught off guard. I thought I'd have more time before he woke up.

"What?" I ask. "Me?"

"I don't see anybody else here at the moment," he says, chuckling.

"Right," I say, lowering Anges' phone and sliding it under my blanket.

I don't want to sneak around and hide what I'm doing from Puck, but I need to see more. I've only just begun to learn what's happening out in the world.

"Did you sleep well?" Puck asks.

It doesn't sound like he noticed the phone. Thank God. He pulls his phone out of his pocket and quickly looks over a few things. I assume he's checking for messages from his-- *our*-- important people. It doesn't take him long to close the phone and return it to his pocket. All must be well.

"Yeah, I slept like a rock," I say. "Looked like you did, too. I guess we both needed the rest."

Pucks stretches, smiling. He sits up in the chair and rests his feet on the floor. I'm surprised he isn't sore after sleeping in such a contorted position. It doesn't seem to have fazed him. Even uninjured, I'm not sure I could have gotten any shut eye twisted up like Puck was.

"I guess so. You need help going to the bathroom again?"

I shake my head. "Agnes helped me. She's already been here."

"Well, look at you," he says. "I didn't hear her come in. But I'm proud of you, kiddo. You keep that up, and you'll be discharged before you know it. I know you want to blow this popsicle stand."

Puck's encouragement warms me. I lean my head back and smile big, laughing at his popsicle stand comment. Another example of his lovable dorkiness. He has the dad jokes all queued up and ready, apparently.

"Won't that be the day?"

"I'll bet it will happen soon," Puck adds. "Have you asked when you can go home?"

I shake my head again. "No, I haven't. But I should. Dr. Khatri should be coming to check on me sometime this morning. I'll ask him when I see him. I do feel a lot stronger than I did yesterday. I just wish I could take a shower. I feel gross."

"There's a shower in there, right?" he asks.

"I think so, yeah."

"Do you have clothes to put on? That might help you feel better. More… human, you know? If it were me, I'd rather wear my own clothes than a hospital gown."

"I don't think so," I say. "You were going to get my bag from Margot, remember?"

"Oh, yeah, I do," he replies. "My bad. I got so caught up in the drama with the smoke down the block and the alarms blaring. Then there was your drawing for Detective Marsh. I didn't want to leave you here alone. And then I fell asleep… So, here we are."

"It's okay."

"I'll get your bag, though. Want me to bring a few

changes of clean clothes for you? I could run and get them now. I'd be back in a jiffy."

"In a jiffy?" I ask, teasing.

"Hey, hey," he replies. "Don't make fun of my peculiar phrases. I don't make fun of your Wisconsin accent."

I pretend to be shocked by his comment. "*I* have a Wisconsin accent? I don't know what you're talking about."

Puck raises his brows and looks at me in mock disbelief. We both know I definitely have a Wisconsin accent. I've tried to adapt to the way Floridians sound since leaving my home state and arriving on Hideaway Isle, but I doubt I'll ever get rid of my accent entirely. I'm aware that I round out consonants and drag out vowels. My tone is nasally. And I sometimes make "t" sounds more like "d" sounds. It's just what I do. I can't help it.

"Fine," I say. "In a jiffy would be great, Puck. Can you bring some shampoo, a toothbrush and toothpaste, and deodorant? The home stuff is way better than what they have here at the hospital. The keys to my RV were in my bag."

"Yeah, no problem at all," he replies. "I'm sure Margot has whatever you may need, anyway."

"You expect to reach Margot this morning?"

I can tell this catches him off guard.

"What?"

Puck pauses, collecting his thoughts. I can tell he doesn't want to lie to me, just like I don't want to lie to him about the phone in my lap.

"I guess I don't know for sure that I'll be able to reach her," he says. "I'm hoping. And that's the truth, Basia. I hope to reach her. I know she'll want to come and see you. Rags, too."

I narrow my eyes, assessing his statement.

"What about Lottie?" I ask.

Puck stands and shoves his hands into his pockets. I'm making him nervous.

"Oh, well, I don't know," he says. "Maybe I'll reach Margot and maybe she'll have some new information."

"Yeah?"

"Yeah. I promise to share with you when there's something new to share," he says.

I can tell he's choosing his words carefully. I hate it. But I want Puck to get on his way so I can continue my search on Agnes' phone, so I let it go.

"I appreciate that," I say. "I'll be here waiting when you get back."

His body relaxes. He's relieved that I won't press the subject-- for now. He knows this conversation is far from over.

"Are you sure you're okay with me leaving you here alone for a bit? I could bring back breakfast. Are you allowed to eat solid foods?"

I shrug. "I don't know, but a sausage biscuit sounds amazing. Can you bring me one? With orange juice and a side of hash browns? That would be dreamy."

"Happy to," Puck replies. "I'll bring it in. Even if you can't eat it right away, it will keep awhile. We can always heat it up at the nurses' station. I'm pretty sure they have a microwave back there."

"Good," I say.

I don't mention the explosions or my newfound knowledge that yesterday's blast wasn't the only one. I also don't say anything about Tom Marsh or my drawing. There will be time to discuss those things later. At the moment, I have a one-track mind.

Puck gives me a hug, then excuses himself, promising to be back within a couple of hours. He says he'll stop home and grab a shower himself so he can see Chely for a little while. I don't mind. I'm glad he's tending to his own needs. I'll probably stay busy while he's gone, anyway. The time will pass quickly.

I eye the sketchpad on the table beside my bed. Puck left it for me. My hands are beginning to feel heavy again, like they want to draw something. I think I'll let them, just as soon as I'm done with Agnes' phone. She'll want it back soon, no doubt. Without wasting another minute, I pull the phone back out and navigate to the local news again.

From the main menu, I find the list of featured stories, but I don't start there this time. Instead, I go to the search bar and type in what I'm really after: Lottie Callaway. My eyes widen as I hit enter and a long list of articles appear, all with Lottie's name highlighted. Some have her name in the headline. Others don't mention her until the body of the text. My heart races as I scan them. I didn't realize there would be so many.

I guess I should have expected a lot of results due to the drama with Lottie's boat tour company, Island Boat Tours. People died, and in the wake of the tragedy there are angry loved ones who claim Lottie was negligent. Maybe she was, but I know her intentions were good. If you ask me, she got in over her head. She didn't have the experience needed to properly handle such a venture. She is responsible for what happened, at least, partially. My opinion doesn't change my love for Lottie, though. I stand by her. I know she isn't a mean person. She didn't wish death on innocent people, that's for sure.

Focusing my attention on the search results on the newspaper's website, the first entry startles me. My eyes don't want to focus as I read Lottie's name alongside the word arrested.

"No!" I say out loud, even though I'm alone in the room. "No, no, no!"

The latch on the door clanks, then suddenly, Puck's face appears.

"No what?" he asks.

He looks down and sees the phone in my hands.

"Oh," he adds reluctantly. "I was coming back to tell you that Herbert plans to…"

Puck doesn't finish his sentence. I look up at him, my face a ball of confusion and anger. I don't try to hide the phone in my hands this time. To the contrary, I look back down at it and begin to read the article, ignoring whatever it is he wants to tell me about Herbert. I doubt Puck's message is more serious than Lottie having been arrested.

Springing into action, Puck darts toward me, and for a minute I think he'll try to take the phone out of my hands.

"Basia…" he begins.

"Don't talk to me," I say. "I'm busy."

He stops short of actually leaping onto my bed, but he gets close enough to the side of it to see what I'm reading.

"Basia, please, don't be mad," Puck pleads.

I hadn't even said that I was mad. His response is

telling. There must be a reason to be mad. They must have known about Lottie's arrest all along. Which means they kept it from me on purpose. Thank God for Agnes believing I deserved to know the truth.

"So, that's why Lottie is missing, yet no one is terribly concerned about looking for her. Except that *you* said Margot and Rags were looking for her. What the fuck, Puck? Did you lie to me? How could you?"

I am pissed. My voice is loud. I hear it, and I know that it's too loud for this hospital setting, but I'm upset.

"We didn't lie to you," he tries. "We just withheld some information…"

"We?" I ask. "So, you are all in on it together. How many of you? Herbert, too?"

"Basia, calm down," he says. "We did it on the advice of your doctor."

"Dr. Khatri?" I ask in disbelief. "He wouldn't…"

A calmer me would completely understand. In fact, I've already thought about this type of scenario and I get why the doctors would have wanted to avoid allowing me to get worked up. There was a bleed on my brain. And I imagine it might have gotten worse if my emotions had caused more blood to pump, when that was the last thing that needed to happen. But now? What's Puck's excuse for sitting here with me-- for hours-- and not mentioning it. Or Margot and Rags' excuse for not coming to see me and telling me all about the true story of my girlfriend's arrest. At what point does their careful treatment of me become wrong? At what point can I no longer trust them?

Puck nods. "Yes, Dr. Khatri. On the day of your surgery-- which was the day of your injury-- Lottie's arrest was all over the news. The doctor saw it himself.

He told us in no uncertain terms that your surgery was going to be touch and go. He told us that your chances of survival were fifty-fifty at best. He knew you were agitated, asking for Lottie. He didn't want you upset."

"No…"

"But he did!" Puck says, desperate for me to believe him. "I promise you, Basia. Dr. Khatri is the one who made this decision for us. You're my friend. I'd never hurt you. I was only acting in what I thought was your best interest. And the same goes for the rest of the group. Not one of us would hurt you. We care about you very much. *I swear.*"

I cross my arms over my chest, a protective move. I don't want to hear any of this. I don't want it to be true. And I don't know how to reconcile my anger with what Puck's telling me. Right now, I'm even angry at Dr. Khatri. Agnes is, apparently, the only one truly on my side.

"If that's true, then tell me now!" I shout.

Agnes has removed all the monitors from my body, so there's no beeping machine to keep pace with my heart, but I can feel my pulse quicken. I toss the phone in my lap, ready to hear the details from Puck instead of reading them online.

He shakes his head, then rams his fingers through his disheveled hair. If I weren't so mad, I might feel bad for him. But right now, I don't. I just want answers.

"What do you want to know?" he asks, plopping down into a chair. "Maybe I should ask what you've already read online?"

"That Lottie isn't missing. She hasn't been taken. And she hasn't run away. She was *arrested*, of all things."

"Okay," Puck says. "Did you read far enough to learn why?"

I hate that I can't say yes. I'm tired of being at everyone else's mercy.

"No, I didn't," I reply. "I was about to, but you barged in and interrupted me."

The word barged is dramatic, I admit. I'm not being fair to Puck. I'm just too mad, and I have to get the frustration out somehow.

"Well, do you want to know?" he asks.

"Yes!" I say. "Get on with it, already."

"Okay, okay," Puck says. He leans forward, resting his elbows on his knees, then looks me squarely in the eye. "If you're ready. It may be upsetting."

"I am," I say. "Was it the boat tour accident? Have they brought charges against her?"

"I wish it were that simple," Puck said. "But you aren't far off the mark there. Charges are pending in that incident. The police have said they intend to charge Lottie with manslaughter. I think the way they worded it was that the charges were due to her misconduct, negligence and inattention to her duties. The captain of the boat who was on board the day of the accident is supposedly being charged, too."

"That's horrible," I say. "But we can get her a good lawyer. She can fight this. She did her best. It was an accident."

"I understand," Puck says. "But that's not all. I mean… it's not the only charge she's facing. It's not the only thing Lottie *did*."

20

PASSION PEOPLE

Gently, Puck puts a hand on my knee to offer his support. I could both smack him and hug him. I'm a tangled mess of emotions.

"What else?" I ask. "What did Lottie do? You have to tell me."

He takes a long, slow breath.

"I wish this hadn't fallen on my shoulders," he says. "I wish Margot was here to show you. She's sort of the unofficial leader of the family, and…"

"This isn't about you, Puck. But wait. What do you mean show me?" I ask. "Is there video? Of what?"

He nods, then opens his phone. With a few swipes, Puck has YouTube queued up and is handing me the device. YouTube. Damn. Not even a news outlet. Whatever this is has probably already spread far and wide. I take the phone out of his hands eagerly, then push play. I steel myself. I have no idea what I'm going to see. It can't possibly be good.

In a flash, I find out. It's cell phone footage of the day

I was injured. Whoever filmed this started when Nigel was getting loud. It's jarring to watch our scuffle from this vantage point. I can feel the fear again as I see myself on camera, first trying to avoid confrontation, then moving to protect Lottie. Tears stream down my face as I watch. I couldn't stop the tears if I tried, so I let them flow freely. On video, I see the blow to the back of my head that knocked me out. I see myself collapse onto the restaurant's patio, and then finally, I see what happened after.

The footage feels like it's in slow motion as I watch, my life and future wrapped up in the outcome of events I wasn't privy to. It's a strange experience. Seconds after I hit the ground, Nigel kicks his head back and laughs like a jackal. What a prick. I'm blacked out, and he thinks it's funny. I'd like to give him the benefit of the doubt and say that maybe he didn't realize the seriousness of my injuries, but I think he's just an asshole. Plain and simple. At first, Lottie is on the ground with me. I knocked her down as I collapsed. She tends to me, crying and kissing my face, begging me to wake up. It's hard to watch. Margot and Rags rush to my side. They begin checking my pulse and my airway, making sure I remain stable until medics arrive.

I glance away from the video for a moment and up at Puck. "This is brutal," I mumble.

"I know. I'm sorry. Keep watching," he says. "Almost there."

I turn back to the screen, beginning to understand what must have happened. I watch Lottie's expression as she narrows her eyes and glares at Nigel. She glances down at my limp body, exasperated, then stands to face him again. In what seems like a hastily calculated move, Lottie looks around at the mess of broken glasses and dinner plates that crashed to the ground during the altercation. Quickly, she finds what she's searching for. Picking up a beer bottle, she breaks it against the edge of a table, then grips her newfound weapon. The look of determination in my girlfriend's eyes is frightening, yet I'm proud of her for being brave. She apparently didn't cower from Nigel. Not once. Not even when he knocked me out.

The video footage continues as Lottie surges forward, weapon in hand. She approaches Nigel at top speed, then shoves the broken beer bottle straight into his soft neck. She gets it in there deep. Nigel reels, teetering on shaky legs. He's too shocked to defend himself against the blow. Instantly, blood spurts from the young man's neck, cascading down his torso and legs. Nigel wasn't expecting that from Lottie, that's for sure. He thought he had the upper hand. He falls to the ground, a look of horror on his face.

From there, the scene becomes complete chaos. Rags shelters Lottie when Nigel's friend goes after her. Margot covers me and doesn't let anyone get too close. Whoever is doing the filming moves back, apparently afraid to get caught up in the turbulent scene. Within another minute, sirens wail in the distance and rapidly draw nearer. Police swarm the scene, then ambulances. Even a fire truck shows up, for good measure, before the video ends. As the screen goes black, I notice the number of views: 4.6 million already.

"Holy shit," I mumble.

"Yeah," Puck replies. "You're sort of… I don't know, internet famous."

"I didn't ask to be," I say.

"I realize that," Puck says softly. His shoulders slump with the weight of what he's telling me. "Basia, they're holding Lottie on charges of aggravated assault with a deadly weapon."

My face flushes upon hearing this news. The combination of charges from the boat tour accident and now this doesn't bode well for Lottie joining me in our old lives anytime soon. It sounds like she's in a lot of serious trouble.

"But this thing with Nigel was self-defense. Wasn't it?"

Puck shrugs. "I'm no lawyer. Or police officer. I don't know."

"It was definitely a crime of passion. Lottie was upset because of my injury, which almost cost me my life. It's better for her defense that way, right? It isn't like she just decided to go after Nigel and hurt him… unprovoked. She was responding to his assault on me."

"I hear you," he says.

"What happened to him?"

"Nigel?"

"Yes," I say. "Who else?"

Puck purses his lips. "I don't know for sure what his current status is, Basia, but he's here, in this hospital. At least, he was…"

My eyes widen when I hear this. I wonder if Dr. Khatri has been taking care of Nigel, too. I don't know how to feel about that. On one hand, I hate Nigel for what he did to us, and I might like for him to die. It sounds cruel, but it's the truth. If he dies, then he'd be out of our way. And maybe it would be fair and just, given what he did to me. On the other hand, I can't actually bring myself to wish death on anyone. Even Nigel. Even after everything. I just don't have it in me. I'm a believer in man's ability to learn and grow. To do better once we know better.

"He's alive?" I ask.

"He *was* alive," Puck confirms. "Last I heard. I know he was brought here with life-threatening injuries. His dad came down from Wisconsin and made a statement to one of the TV news stations out of Miami. No more information has been released to the public since. That was days ago now."

"Nigel Senior?" I ask.

"Yeah, that's him," Puck confirms. "Did you know them? I hear you're both from Fox, Wisconsin. You went to the same high school, right?"

"Yeah, Fox Senior High," I confirm. "Nigel was a menace then, too. I guess Lottie showed him who was boss."

I smile just a little. It's wrong of me, but I do it. Nigel harassed so many people at our high school, and that was several years ago. I doubt he's let up. I must admit, I'm proud that it was my Lottie who finally taught him a lesson.

Puck notices that I'm lost in thought. He looks away, out the window. It seems like he wants to give me privacy. It also seems like he's waiting to see if I'm still mad at him. I am.

"What does all of this mean as related to the explosions?" I ask once I'm ready to talk some more.

"You know there was more than one explosion?" Puck asks.

"Yes, I read it. Before I searched for Lottie's name. Well, before you woke up, actually." He looks surprised but remains low-key. "The article said there have been five in total," I add.

"Yeah, it's getting bad out there," Puck replies.

I nod. "So, what does it have to do with Lottie?"

"I'm not sure it has anything to do with her," Puck says. "Maybe you should ask Tom about that. He'd know better than I would."

"Maybe I should ask Tom," I agree. "But he's not here right now and I want to talk this through. I'd say you owe me a few more minutes of your time to…"

"Okay, okay," Puck says. "True."

He rubs his temples, trying to think. I do the same, as if the duplicate motions will activate some sort of twin powers like in the old cartoons Pa used to watch with me. I wish it were that easy. I close my eyes, going back in my mind to all the mental work I did while in the ICU. I review the possible connections I'd come up with, and I compare them against the new information I've learned.

Before I can decipher anything useful, a loud boom rocks us. It's even louder than the one that happened yesterday. It's so loud and powerful that it shakes my entire body, making me feel like a ragdoll. When the shaking stops, Puck and I look at each other.

"That was close," he says. "Closer than yesterday."

I nod. Sure enough, the hospital alarm sounds again, complete with the flashing white light.

"Lockdown," Puck and I say in unison.

"Look outside!" I shout. "See if there's smoke."

Puck nods back, then rushes to the window. He presses his cheek against the glass, looking in the opposite direction from where the smoke was before.

"I see it," he says. "Black smoke, just like yesterday. Only this time, it's in the opposite direction. And it's definitely closer to the hospital. I can't tell for sure, but it looks like it might be right next door."

"What's next door?" I ask. "Is there an abandoned building?"

"I don't know," Puck says. "I didn't notice one."

He lowers his brow as he thinks.

"Close your eyes," I instruct. "See it in your mind's eye. You can remember. You came in that way, didn't you?"

He nods quickly, then does as I ask. There's a sense of urgency that we didn't have before. This is getting scary, especially considering how my hunch tells me Lottie's situation is somehow connected to the blasts.

"I remember!" Puck says. "I see it."

"Okay, what's there?" I ask eagerly.

He shakes his head, like he doesn't want it to be true. "It's… I'm pretty sure it's the parking garage."

I gasp. I suspected there would be people injured this time, but I didn't think it would be visitors to the hospital. That's a vulnerable group to begin with.

"Oh, no," I say.

We stare at each other for a moment as the alarm blares in the background. Neither of us know what to do. We're largely powerless here, yet we both want to help. How? The answer isn't clear.

Suddenly, I have the overwhelming urge to sketch on the pad. It's as if my life depends on it. I feel like I might literally burst if I don't let whatever this is out and onto the paper.

"Quick!" I say. "Hand me the sketchpad and a pencil. Please!"

"On it," Puck says. He practically leaps over the chair between him and the pad, eager to be useful. "Here! Do your thing, my friend."

I smile at Puck, and I realize I'm not mad anymore. Not really. I'm disappointed, and I'm unhappy about having things kept a secret from me, but I don't blame any of my people. Like Puck said, they were following Dr. Khatri's orders, doing what they all thought was best for me. I guess when you get right down to it, I'm mad at the situation. Not at Puck. Or Margot, Rags, or Herbert. The difficult situation is to blame. If anyone is at fault, it's Nigel. Sounds like he got what was coming to him, though, so I can't really even be mad at him.

"Thank you," I say, but I don't start drawing right away. "Puck, do you mind giving me some time alone with this sketch pad?"

He looks confused. "Sure, except the alarms… and the lockdown. I don't think I can leave."

"You can leave this room, even if you can't leave the hospital," I say.

"But… where will I go?"

Funny how Puck was all ready to go home and check on Chely before. He must be spooked by the latest explosion. I don't blame him. It's scary. It's just that I have drawing to do. I'm too focused on that task to be very afraid.

"How about you go find Tom?" I ask. "I have a

feeling that I'll soon have something important to show him."

"Okay," Puck replies. "Right. I'll call Tom. They'll probably let him in, even with the lockdown."

"Probably," I agree.

I smile again, patiently, as I wait for Puck to take his leave. I can practically feel my fingers pulled to the pad, but I restrain them. This is something I want to do alone. I can't explain why, but I feel it deep in my bones. Puck seems hesitant to go, but finally, he does. He gives a sheepish wave as he slides out the door and then closes it gently behind him. Once the door latches and I'm by myself, I move like a madwoman, all grabbing hands and flying fingers as I draw the scenes pouring out of my soul.

I pause briefly, closing my eyes to let the flow of energy move through me unencumbered. When I do, an interesting thing happens. The celestial music I heard at the sanctuary with Charmiene becomes audible again. The angelic melody surrounds me, and I use it to press forward, opening my eyes and bringing myself in earnest to the paper. The beautiful music drowns out the alarm, so I barely hear the harsh alert tones anymore. I feel enveloped in love and support, much like I did in the garden with Pa. If I didn't know better, I'd think Charmiene was in the room with me right now. Her presence feels so safe, so familiar, that I wonder if she hasn't been with me all along. Maybe she really is my own personal guardian angel.

For what feels like hours, I draw. Time does the same wonky thing it did during my previous visit with Charmiene, and I can't tell what's what. It almost feels like time is irrelevant in this mode, in this flow. I keep drawing, even as Agnes pokes her head in to check on me. Even when the alarms stop and then start again. Nothing fazes me. I draw one sketch after another, barely paying attention to the finished product. When one is done, I feel it in my gut. Only then do I turn the page and begin anew. My fingers move so surely, I think I might be possessed. I honestly don't care if I am. Until, in a blessed crescendo of images and music, I place my pencil down on my lap, my work complete.

21

ROAR

I believe it was Mary Anne Radmacher who said one of my favorite quotes about how courage doesn't always roar. She asserts that, sometimes, courage is the little voice at the end of the day that says I'll try again tomorrow. I first heard the quote in Mrs. McClanahan's class, of all places. It has stuck with me. I'm reminded of it now, as I assess my strengths and come to terms with my weaknesses. It's all I can do.

My injury and the experiences since have taught me much. Most of all, they've taught me that I'm not invincible. Like everyone else on this planet, I must work from within the limits of the human body. But that's not a burden, really. It's an opportunity. Life is beautiful. I know that for sure. I could have passed on and stayed in the garden with Pa. Yet I didn't. For that, I'm glad. I intend to do good things here in the land of the living for the rest of my days. Those good things don't have to be loud or physically powerful. I know that now. They can be quiet, subtle, and gentle. That's perfectly okay. They're just as valuable as any other contributions.

When my collection of drawings is done, I rest for a while before Tom shows up to see what I've unearthed. The all-clear is given at the hospital right around the time he arrives, and the alarms stop their incessant beeping. I suspect Tom had been tied up with the matter of the latest explosion, which was why it took him a few hours to arrive after Puck called. That's alright. I feel good about what I've drawn and how it will help investigators on various fronts. Everything in its own time.

Puck stands beside me like a proud big brother as Tom oohs and ahhs over my sketches. Tom snaps photos of every single one. I can tell by his reactions that he recognizes many of the faces I've drawn, even though I don't know most of them. He claims my work will assist multiple detectives in the cases they're working on, including the one related to the recent explosions. I don't ask questions about Llew, Nigel, or Lottie. For some reason, all that drawing made me feel downright serene and peaceful, like everything will be alright. Even obstacles that seem insurmountable-- such as the charges against Lottie-- don't worry me. I feel like they'll work themselves out, in due time.

Before Tom leaves, he offers me a job. I practically leap out of my hospital bed to hug him in thanks. He offers me a full-time position working at the police station as a Special Projects Coordinator. He says I'll be using my drawing medium abilities, but that we can't come right out and make that my job title. He explains that most of what I do for the department will happen behind the scenes. The public won't know details of how I actually work. I'm fine with that. I'm not sure I'd want the public to know. Tom says that after I go through some training, he'll promote me to Special Projects Officer and that I'll have a real badge and everything. One of the best parts of Tom's offer is that after sixty days, I'll have health insurance benefits and paid time off. I can hardly believe it. I didn't think that kind of job and income security would be available to me. I gratefully accept, sealing the deal with a handshake and a promise to start work just as soon as I'm discharged and feel up to it.

I'm pretty sure I glow like a light bulb for the rest of the day. I feel useful in a way I've never experienced before. I like it. It feels like I may have found my calling. Or, at least, one of them. I'm certain this is the next right step for me. Where things go from there will remain to be seen.

Puck finally heads home for that shower and to grab my bag, as promised. He returns with my things as the sun sets and we settle in for another night in my hospital room. This time, I hold my own phone in my hands. I tell Puck that I can stay alone if he wants to go be with Chely, but he insists he isn't going anywhere. I can't thank him enough. I let him stay.

Dr. Khatri checks on me before going home for the day. I don't give him hell about withholding information from me, and I don't ask if he's treating Nigel. I let all that go in favor of focusing on the positive. It feels like the right thing to do. The man saved my life, after all. Gratitude is definitely in order. The doctor says he's pleased with my progress and that if it continues, he will discharge me in the morning. Along with Tom's job offer, that's the best news I've heard in a long time. Things are really beginning to look up for me. After what felt like an excruciatingly long wait, I'm finally able to land where I belong and to make a difference in the world around me in a way that matters.

I wait until the day shift nurse leaves before showering because I only feel comfortable with Agnes helping me. She does, and I thank her profusely for both the shower and for leaving her phone like she did. It was the catalyst that allowed things to break loose for me. I'm grateful. At the end of the night, I fall peacefully asleep. I'm content, even though there's much left to learn and solve.

I know there will be a hard road ahead when it comes to my physical recovery. The type of injury I sustained takes a toll. It will be slow going for a while. I'll have to do physical therapy, and I'll have to take it easy. I won't be able to push myself like I used to. I also know that Lottie has a difficult battle ahead, both legally and with her public image. I intend to be there for her every step of the way. We'll get through it together, the same way Puck and I will get through our bad dreams of shark teeth and nasty wolves together, if they should return. Whatever we face, my friends and I will have each other's backs, always.

Truth be told, I also know our little island will see more explosions before it's over. I hate to think about it, but I suspect the vision I had of the big Miami explosion may come to pass at some point, too, as may the vision of Nigel and his friend being swallowed by the cloud of smoke and debris. I'll keep drawing for Tom and will stay tuned into my intuition. I can only hope I'll receive information that will keep the big one at bay. I'll do my very best to thwart it. My absolute, very best.

As strange as it sounds, my near-death experience

made me realize that even if the worst happens, there's another place waiting for us when we leave here. It's not where any of us want to go before our time, but it's not scary. It's not bad. It's okay. Loved ones on both sides of the veil hold and keep us. If we all focus on being good to each other, we can make it through almost any terrible situation. That's what I choose to believe, anyway. I suspect that belief and focus on the positive is what will keep me going.

When I wake up the next morning, Puck is gone, but Agnes is there with a list of discharge instructions. She goes over them with me, one by one, until she's satisfied that I'll do everything necessary to take care of myself. I'll have to take the walker home with me. I'll also have to report for physical therapy at the hospital three times per week. Agnes tells me in no uncertain terms that head injuries are some of the most serious, and that I must call Dr. Khatri's office or 9-1-1 if I have any of the emergency symptoms listed. I agree, cheerfully, then Agnes helps me get cleaned up for the day. I'm stronger now, so she doesn't have to help me much.

I never thought I'd be so proud to simply care for my own basic needs. Yet here I am. I'm proud. I'll relish my success. Less than a week ago, no one knew if I'd be leaving this hospital in anything other than a body bag. I'll happily claim my progress as a victory. A big, juicy one. One that I'll remember until the day I die. Hopefully, that day won't come until I'm an old woman, satisfied and spent after a life full of the people, places, and things I love most.

Agnes takes the IV out of my hand, and for the first time in a while, I truly feel free.

I wash my face and brush my hair and teeth, then I put on some of the clothes Puck left. They aren't mine, but he said Margot sent them. Margot and I are about the same size, so it works. Margot is more muscular than I am, but her clothes fit. Wearing them makes me feel loved and cared for. I can't wait to see Margot and Rags again.

When I'm dressed, I sit upright in a chair and wait for breakfast. It's another gorgeous day on the island, and the Florida sun shines brightly through the window in my room. I can eat more than broth now, and my appetite is hearty. Agnes tells me the cafeteria workers should be around with a tray soon, but as it turns out, I have a better option on the way.

I can smell the sausage and hashbrowns the minute the door opens. Puck holds a brown paper bag in one hand, the top folded over neatly. A paper cup of what I can only presume is orange juice occupies his other hand.

"Good morning, sunshine," he says with a smile. "A little birdie told me you're going home today."

Puck is showered and ready for the day. He must have slipped out early so he could get back here with my breakfast. That was incredibly nice of him, especially on my discharge day.

"Is that so?" I ask.

"Yep. And Jimmy Buffet is here for it."

I laugh as Puck queues up Margaritaville on his phone and makes us both wear the sunglasses again. We're in full celebration mode, singing and dancing, me with my shoulders and him in full body moves that I don't recommend he try at the club. He doesn't seem to have much sense about his own dorkiness. It's all the more adorable that way. I already love that dorky guy. I hope we stay friends forever. And I hope that one day, Lottie and I will get married, and Puck will officially become my brother-in-law. I like the sound of that.

I scarf down the sausage biscuit and hashbrowns like I'm starving. I guess I am. I'm starving for regular life outside of the hospital. For the good stuff, like cheeseburgers in paradise, cold Wisconsin-brewed beer, hugs from my friends, warm kisses from my girlfriend, a soft bed that doesn't have side rails, and fresh Hideaway Isle air that smells like tall palm trees and the sparkling sea.

I'd like to think that Pa is watching as Puck and I cycle through Jimmy Buffet songs with the enthusiasm of friends who are chock full of life. I hope Pa truly does see that I'm alive and well. I hope he's always around, like he told me he was. I feel light and happy. Having communicated with Pa is a large part of why I feel this way now. Knowing what happened to him healed emotional wounds and cleared away emotional baggage that I didn't even realize I was carrying. It feels so good to set that down.

As I eat, Puck stares at me with a huge grin on his face.

"What are you looking at, dork?" I ask playfully.

He presses his lips together, holding back an even bigger smile. "Nothing!"

Now I'm curious. It seems like it's something.

"No, seriously," I say. "What has you looking like the cat that swallowed the canary?"

He laughs out loud, clearly up to something. I scoot to the edge of my seat, very interested. Whatever it is, it seems good. And it seems like a big deal. Puck glances at his phone, then at the door.

"What are you watching for?" I ask insistently. "Are Margot and Rags coming by? Because that would be a great surprise. I've really missed them."

Puck shrugs, then glances at his phone again.

"Stay here," he says. "I'll be right back."

"Puck…" I begin, but he moves fast and is gone before I can stop him.

He bounds out the door like an excited puppy after a ball. I wonder what in the world he's up to.

Growing up, I shied away from surprises. There was enough disappointment in life that I didn't care to tempt fate, especially since I thought Pa had abandoned me. I was constantly hoping he would come back. I guess that put me in the habit of avoiding the unknown. I didn't believe life could dish out good things, so I focused on keeping my head down in an effort to minimize the bad. That began to change when I met Lottie. I felt so lucky to have met her, and for her to have become my girlfriend. That good fortune was the start of my believing that other good things were possible. And now, well, I feel so free that I just might begin to expect good things.

Within minutes, Puck's back. He bounces in the door, grinning from ear to ear.

"What?" I ask, hardly able to contain my excitement after all the buildup.

"You have a special visitor," he says. My eyes must light up too brightly because he clarifies. "It's not Lottie. I'm sorry. I wish it was. But this is going to be good. I promise."

"Okay," I say, unsure of who it might be.

"Are you ready for someone unexpected?" Puck asks.

I lower my brow. Someone unexpected? Who could that be? Every one of my friends is a member of Lottie's family. They're all one group. And I wouldn't call them unexpected. Sure, I've wished Margot and Rags would visit over the past few days, but it's not a big deal.

"Wait," I say, trying a guess. "Did Chely have the baby?" I sit up straight in my chair at the thought. "Is your little boy here?"

Puck chuckles. "No, that's not it. Chel is still pregnant as can be."

"Then who?" I ask.

Puck puts a hand over his mouth to hold back another giant grin, and his eyes fill with tears.

"Now you're freaking me out," I say. "Would you bring the mystery visitor in already?"

He nods, then opens the door, swinging it wide in dramatic fashion. With the door out of the way, I see a pair of silhouettes. The light in the hallway is brighter than it is in my room, so I can't immediately see their faces, but I do as they step inside. One of the women-- and I can tell for sure they're both women-- is Margot. She's smiling nearly as big as Puck. She's walking arm in arm with the other woman as if they're bridesmaids at a wedding. Although, maybe it's more like Margot is escorting the other woman. The stranger is older. Not old, but older. Rags follows behind them. I can make out his strong frame in the distance.

It takes me a minute. It's disorienting to see the woman here, in this place. Out of place. My mind puts the pieces together just as her face comes into full view. I can hardly believe it. I let out a yelp and tears spring to my eyes with a ferocious intensity.

It's Mama. My very own Mama. Sally Guthrie or Matthews or whatever her last name is these days-- it doesn't matter-- is here. She's here! My mama is here. Her blonde hair is still the same color as mine. She's wearing it in a bun, with a tortoise shell clip as anchor. Pearls frame her collarbones and a silky green blouse billows around her petite frame.

"Hello, Basia," she says through tears of her own.

I'm too choked up to speak and I can't stand up quickly, but I motion for Mama to come to me. She does, and we hug tightly, crying and rocking as we hold onto each other for dear life. She feels so good in my arms. Her gentle touch and her familiar smell soothe me like nothing else could.

"Mama," I finally squeak out. "I'm so glad to see you… So glad you're here. How…?"

She pulls back and looks me in the eyes, smoothing loose strands of hair on the sides of my head like she used to when I was a little girl.

"Honey, I saw the video of what happened to you and I just had to come," she explains.

Mama looks older, but at the same time, still the way she did the day I left.

"How did you…?"

"I called her," Margot says with a smile. "We wanted to bring her here for you. When I reached Sally by phone, she already had her bags packed and was in the process of finding a flight down here. We helped expedite the process."

I shake my head, overwhelmed by the care and

kindness. I've wanted my mama so badly. I didn't think I'd ever see her on this island. I figured I'd have to go home to Wisconsin if I wanted to lay eyes on her again.

"Thank you," I say to Margot. "From the bottom of my heart, thank you."

I mouth the words slowly, drawing them out. I'm taken aback by this whole situation. As good as this is and as happy as I am to see Mama, I worry that if she's seen the video and met Margot, Rags, and Puck, she now knows Lottie is my girlfriend. That means Mama knows I'm gay. And I wonder how she feels about that. I always thought she'd be upset to know, and that she'd disapprove. I want to assume that her presence here means the opposite, but I need to ask. I need her to say the words, so I know for sure.

"Mama," I begin, trying to find my footing. "I have something to ask you."

"Anything, Basia, honey," she says. "I'm just glad you're okay. I've been thinking about you nonstop since you left Wisconsin. And now, I'm so very happy you're okay."

I nod, swallowing hard as I find my nerve. I know I have to spit it out. We have to clear the air.

"Mama," I try again. "The girl in the video… Margot's…"

I can't seem to finish a sentence. The words catch in my throat. My palms begin to sweat. I tell them not to, but they don't listen. Mama sees my distress, then takes my face into both of her hands. I can't look away. She holds me there, my tears soaking her hands. I feel trapped like a caged animal, yet powerful enough to speak my truth.

"The girl… Lottie… She's…"

"Honey, I know," Mama says. "She's your girlfriend."

"Yes," I reply. "But like my *girlfriend* girlfriend. Not just a friend who happens to be a girl. I'm…"

I've thought about speaking these words to Mama for many years. I think about them in bed at night when I can't sleep. I think about them every time a stranger gives me a dirty look for holding Lottie's hand in public. And I think about them each time I consider my future. What I really want is for Mama to accept me for who I am. I want her to tell me it's okay to be myself, exactly as I was made. I'm not sure she's capable of any of that, but at minimum, I want to say the words to her. I want to be out and proud. I want to be me.

"Basia, honey," Mama says again, her hands still cupping my face. "I *know*. You're gay. I've known that since you were in third grade and wanted to marry Felicity Turner. You're my daughter. I love you as you are."

I can't believe it. I didn't have to say the words. Mama came to Hideaway Isle, Florida and said them for me. And now, I know that our fractured relationship can be made whole again. I can tell her about my hopes and dreams. I don't expect her to be perfect. She's flawed, for sure. We all are. But Mama and I have found each other again. I can tell her about Pa. And maybe she can make me some of that chicken soup I'm so fond of. All is right in my world. Not perfect. Not flawless. But right.

"Have room for a few more?" Herbert asks as he peeks his head in the door.

"Of course, Grandpa Herbert," I say.

Mama and I are still hanging onto each other as

Chevelle and Chely follow him in. Except for Lottie, the gang's all here. Agnes joins us, too. We're nothing but smiles.

My life-- my one delicate and precious life-- is good.

THE END.

Basia Guthrie, Margot and Lottie Callaway, Puck Reed, Rags Bertram, and more of your favorite characters return in the third full-length novel in the Hideaway Isle Series.

Get it now:

The Man at Nimbus Marina
Hideaway Isle - Book Three

Read the prequel short story for free when you sign up for Kelly Utt's email newsletter at kellyutt.com.

Sign up now:

The Boy on Sunset and Main
Hideaway Isle - Prequel

ENJOY THIS BOOK?

A note from Author Kelly Utt

Honest reviews of my books help bring them to the attention of other readers.

If you've enjoyed this book, I would be very grateful if you could spend just five minutes leaving a review (it can be as short as you like) on the book's product page where you purchased and on Goodreads or BookBub.

Thank you very much.

ABOUT THE AUTHOR

Standards of Starlight Books

Kelly Utt

Kelly Utt writes emotional novels for readers who enjoy both suspense and sentimentality. She was born in Youngstown, Ohio in 1976.

Kelly grew up with a dad who would read a book on a weighty topic, ask her to read it, too, and then insist they discuss it together, igniting her passion for life's big questions. That passion is often reflected inKelly's novels, giving them a depth which leaves readers wanting more and thinking about her stories long after the last lines are read.

Kelly holds a Bachelor's degree in psychology from

the University of Tennessee, Knoxville and she studied graduate-level interactive media at Quinnipiac University.

She lives in Nashville, Tennessee with her husband and sons. She also writes romance as Corena Kelly.

www.kellyutt.com

Made in the USA
Columbia, SC
29 November 2021

50011829R00143